WRAPPED
up in you

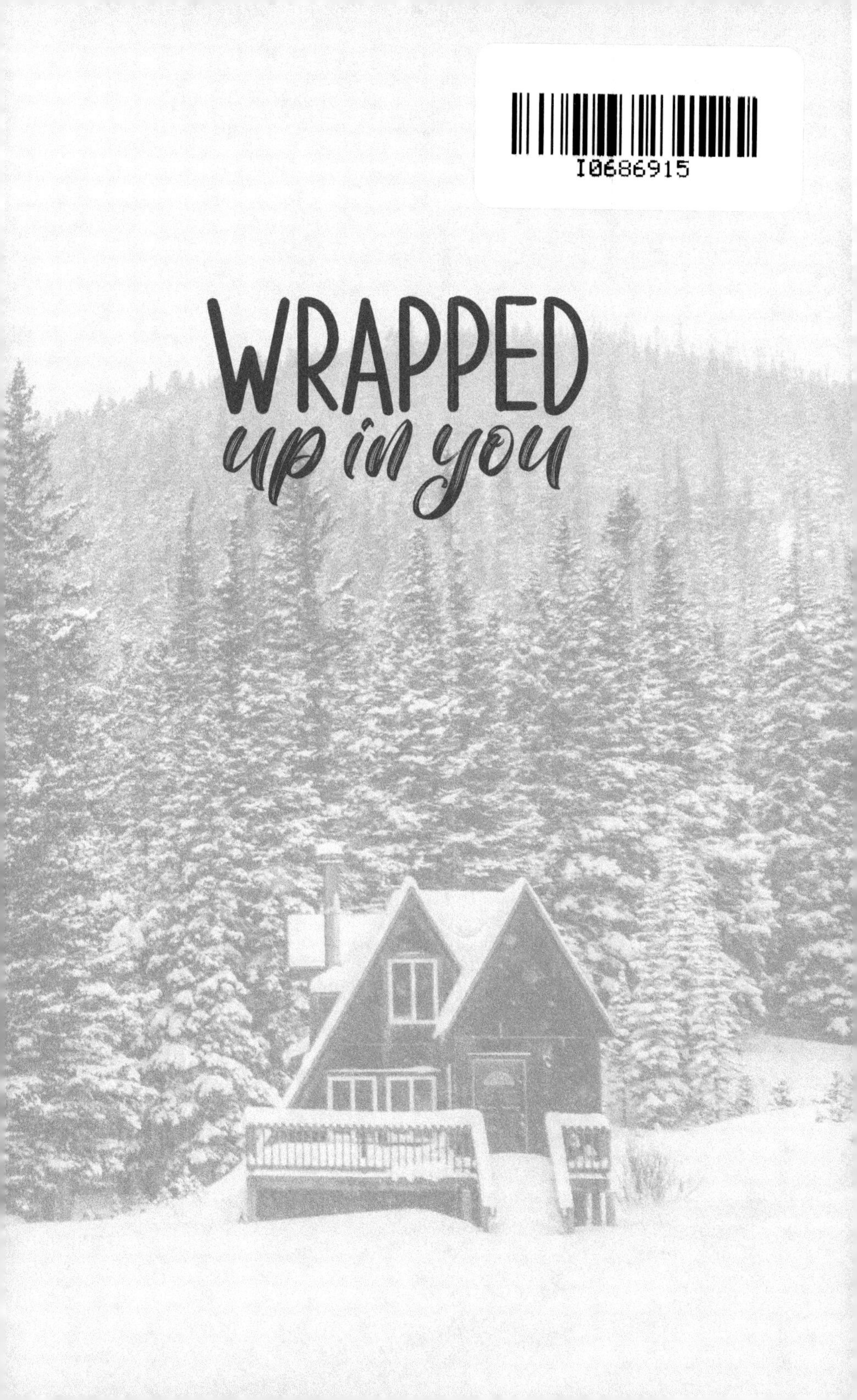

WRAPPED
up in you

D. VESSA

Sometimes you need a change of scenery to figure out what you want in life. Take the damn vacation.

CONTENTS

PLAYLIST

She Knows It | Steven Rodriguez

Heads Carolina, Tails California | Jo Dee Messina

That Don't Impress Me Much | Shania Twain

A Nonsense Christmas | Sabrina Carpenter

Love Gets Me Every Time | Shania Twain

The Right Kind of Wrong | LeAnn Rimes

Santa , Can't You Hear Me | Kelly Clarkson, Ariana Grande

One Way Ticket (Because I Can) LeAnn Rimes

Santa Baby | Ariana Grande, Liz Gillies

Got Me Runnin' Round | Nickelback

Neon Moon| Brooks & Dunn

Like You Mean It | Steven Rodriguez

Amazed | Lonestar

Ain't Nothing 'Bout You | Brooks & Dunn

Waitin' On a Woman | Brad Paisley

CHAPTER
One

WYNN

H ave you ever felt like if you didn't get away right this second, you'd have a full-blown breakdown and probably end up on a grippy-sock-mandatory vacation? Because that's exactly where I am in life right now.

I think I have about one good blow left in me before I have no more fucks left. There won't be anything else to give either, because I'm all used up. Between a boss that doesn't think a bronchitis diagnosis from a doctor is a good enough excuse to miss work and being alone for yet another holiday. Sorry, but my voice sounding like nails on a chalkboard isn't exactly good for business, Gary.

The sad thing is that Christmas used to be my favorite holiday. My mom would decorate the house until it looked like she had thrown up tinsel everywhere, and you were one Christmas song away from throwing the speakers out the window. It was always just her and me until it wasn't. Now that I'm an adult, I realize she only did all of that to fill the void of family.

God, do I miss her.

It's a different kind of loneliness to have people in your life and still feel alone. All of my friends invited me to their Christmas but honestly, that just makes everything worse. Their presence throws what you lack and desperately desire in your face, forcing you to pretend you aren't internally suffering.

I know they were all shocked when I denied the invitations. Even more shocked when they found out my actual plans. They all thought I was crazy that I rented a cabin I found listed online in Northern Michigan. A place I have never been before, let alone know anything about.

The first picture sold me on the place. It showed the house at the end of a snow-covered drive. The A-frame log cabin sat surrounded by pine trees. A soft glow coming from the windows made it feel homey in a way where I knew I wouldn't feel alone, even if it's just for a vacation. It made me want to curl up inside next to a warm fire with a good book and forget the world.

So, I booked it without looking at any of the pictures of the interior or what town it was in. If there's enough snow to make it look like the Hallmark channel came and vomited their holiday spirit all over, it's good enough for me.

It didn't matter how many bedrooms or bathrooms it had, because it's just me. I'm hoping that, for once in my life, I will be able to just breathe.

So, I packed my car full of clothes and a few presents I had wrapped for myself and took off. I may have gone a little overboard on the clothes, but I didn't know what to bring. The coldest it gets where I live in Virginia is in the thirties, and even then, it's not horrible because it's always humid. And if it does happen to snow, it's a light dusting that melts away by the next week.

It was always a dream of my mom's to have a snowy Christmas. I think it bothered her that she was never able to get us out of the shitty town I grew up in. She never got to see me leave. From time to time, I wonder if she would be proud of how far I've come.

Maybe there's a small part of me that's also doing this trip for her. Every year, I try to do something small to keep her memory alive because as each year passes, she becomes more of a distant memory, and I hate it.

I already looked up a Christmas tree farm nearby. I just want something small and… real. Something I can throw tinsel at and pretend she's here.

Here's to hoping this vacation is everything I've made it out to be in my head.

I crossed the state line into Michigan two hours ago, and my GPS says I still have about another two and a half hours until I reach the cabin. I thought doing a long road trip by myself would be fun and adventurous, but I'm thinking I bit off more than I can chew.

I didn't know you could drive in one state for so long because, from looking at the map, I still have a long fucking way to go. The snow is coming down heavier the further north I drive, landing in thick, white fluff balls. It packs into the potholes where you don't think it's as deep as it is until you drive over it and cringe as you dive down into it.

My poor car.

My ass is numb from sitting in the car for so long. I'd love to be one of those people who stop multiple times along the way, but my brain just doesn't work that way. It's a race between me and the GPS on who can get to the final destination the fastest, and I always win. I've only stopped twice since I left my place almost eight hours ago.

I'm thinking I might need to make one more small pit stop. The crispy coke I sucked down when I stopped at McDonald's for lunch is about to burst out of me. Turning up the radio, I try to drown out the pressure in my bladder.

I make it about another hour and a half before I'm about to burst. I just passed a sign that says the Michigan Welcome Center is ten miles out and has bathrooms.

Who the fuck puts a welcome center with a rest stop in the middle of a state? Not that I'm complaining because I need to stop, but I would think they would want the welcome sign when you cross the state line, not in the middle of nowhere.

The snow is coming down even more aggressively now. I'm not able to drive over 30mph for fear of ending up in a ditch like a few of the cars I've passed. The weather has turned the last hour of my drive into almost three. If I didn't have to keep two hands on the wheel to make myself feel like it's the only way I'm not sliding off the road, I'd be stabbing my eye out with my McDonald's straw.

You can't lose feeling in your ass permanently, right? At this point, it's past tingles and full free-for-all if you wanted to touch it because I wouldn't even feel it.

I feel like a grandma, with both of my hands clenched around the wheel as I lean forward, as if that will magically allow me to see through the blizzard happening around me. It doesn't help that it's pitch black out.

I'm second-guessing all of my life choices. Whose great idea was this? The more I'm thinking about it, it's pretty fucking stupid of me to show up at a random rental in the dark and pray to God that the owner left the keys under the mat like they said.

If I ever make it there.

My anxiety is rising the more time that gets added to my GPS. I don't think I'm winning today.

My stomach shoots into my throat as I reach my exit and hit a patch of black ice. I see my life flash before my eyes as I hit the brakes. But all I can do is try to correct the wheel and pray I don't go into a ditch or hit someone. I'm sliding along the ramp with no control, quickly approaching the stop sign I know I'm going to blow through. Squeezing my eyes shut, I scream as I turn the wheel onto the road, praying a car isn't coming.

I must be off the ice because my brakes work, slamming me back into my seat as my car screeches to a stop.

"Holy shit," I exhale, one of my hands leaving the wheel and going to my chest, trying to stop my heart from beating right out of it.

I swear to God if I die trying to live out my late mom's Hallmark fantasy, I will come back and haunt everyone.

Trust that I have a fucking list. And it's extensive. Basically, I'm Ryan from The Office.

Glancing at my GPS, I see that I'm only twenty minutes from the rental. At this rate, it's probably going to be more like an hour.

Taking a deep breath, and placing both hands back on the wheel, I let my foot off the brake and continue my trek to my destination. The farther I drive, the creepier it gets.

I'm out in the middle of nowhere, surrounded by nothing but trees that look like they go on for miles. It's the perfect spot for a murder, and it doesn't help to have every single Forensic Files episode that I've seen flashing through my mind.

There are no street lamps guiding my way, giving it an eerie feeling. I keep looking in my rearview mirror to check the backseat to make sure someone isn't going to jump out at me.

It's official: this holiday season is making me lose it.

The robotic voice on my GPS tells me I have a left-hand turn coming up in 800 feet. There's a single lamp that's flickering, hanging above the intersection that's strung between two poles. Other than that, I would have blown right past it. Gently pressing on the brakes, I take the turn at a painstaking slow pace. Five more minutes and I'm pulling into a drive that doesn't look like a drive.

There's a short wooden fence with an opening showing where the drive should be, heading straight toward a garage. If there weren't a solid foot of snow on the ground, I'm sure it would look different.

"You could have at least left a light on," I grumble as I take in what I can see of the cabin as I get out of my car, stretching my arms above my head and cringing as I hear my bones pop.

People aren't lying when they say everything on your body feels like it's breaking once you turn thirty. Some days I can barely get out of bed.

Slamming my car door shut, I turn the flashlight on my phone on and head for the trunk to get my bag with my clothes out. I'll worry about the rest tomorrow when I can actually see what the fuck I'm doing.

"Someone hasn't plowed the path to the door," I mutter, juggling my phone to light the way and lifting my fifty-pound suitcase since rolling it through the snow is impossible.

I guess if the owner had plowed, the snow falling so hard would have covered it.

I let out the most unattractive grunts as I haul my suitcase up the steps to the deck that spans the entire front of the A-frame cabin, heading straight for the mat that's partially covered in snow resting in front of the front door.

Having no choice but to stick my bare hand in the snow to lift the mat, I eventually find the key the owner said would be here.

"It's about damn time," I tell the door as I turn the key in the lock. It took me a few tries before I got it, my fingers already feeling a little frozen from not being used to this weather.

I want nothing more than to shower off this day and climb into bed and read a book where I hope to regain feeling in my ass.

Turning the light off on my phone, I place it in my back pocket. Using both hands, I drag my bag inside, letting it drop on the floor with a bang. Just as I'm about to turn around to find a light switch, a lamp in the opposite corner of the room illuminates, revealing a man resembling a grizzly bear.

"What the fuck?" the grizzly bear man thunders out. "Did you

5

seriously break into my place?"

A blood-curdling scream leaves my lips as my hand jumps to my chest, to keep my heart from pounding out of my body for the second time today. Because what the fuck is right.

CHAPTER Two

WYNN

I can't move, let alone think of a response.

Who is this burly man and why is he in the cabin I rented?

I should be freaking out more than I am.

And maybe throw something at his face that looks like it wants to throw me out on my ass.

Didn't I just think about how I could easily end up on the next episode of Forensic Files on my drive here?

Apparently, all sanity has flown out the window.

All I can do is stare at the man in front of me, who is wearing nothing but a pair of gray sweatpants that outline everything. And I mean everything.

His shoulders are broad and thick, just like his arms and chest. Tattoos are scattered across his body, or what I can see of it.

Jesus Christ is there a lot to see.

I've never found chest hair attractive, but it looks neatly trimmed and sexy as hell on him.

God, he's just so burly.

Just like all those men you see chopping wood in the videos online.

That's the only way to describe him.

A big, burly man.

"Are you going to answer me or just stare at me with your

mouth open all night?" he asks angrily, snapping me out of my lumberjack-induced coma.

Picking my jaw up off the floor, my hands go to my hips as one cocks out. If there's one thing to learn about me, it's that I not only match energy, I'll take it to the next level.

"Excuse me?" It takes everything in me not to cock my head, too. Breathing in and out, I try to keep a lid on it, but it feels like I'm failing as my blood pressure rises.

"Excuse me?" he repeats, his brows rising to his hairline as he points a large finger at himself before turning it on me. "You're the one who just broke into my place. Now, I'll repeat what the fuck?"

"I didn't break into your house!" I say, my voice rising with every syllable.

"Uh, from where I'm standing, babe, it looks like you did."

Holding the key to this place up in my hand, I wave it in front of us. "I literally have the key to this place. I don't know the textbook definition of breaking into something, but I bet it doesn't involve me having the key to it."

His scowl deepens as he stalks toward me. My breath catches in my throat as I remain frozen in place. He stops two feet from me before snatching the key I'm still dangling in the air right out of my hands.

"Hey!" I exclaim. "That's my key!"

"Wrong. It's my fucking key. I'm going to give you thirty seconds to explain where you got a key to my place and why you're standing in my fucking living room before I'm calling the cops."

"No, you're wrong," I bite out, stepping toward him and poking him in the chest. Holy shit, my finger basically hit a brick wall. "I rented this place for two weeks, which means it's mine for that duration of time."

He looks down at the spot my finger poked him and back up to me. "You've got the wrong place."

"If I got the wrong place, then how did I get the key that opens it, genius?" I ask, my tone dripping with attitude.

My restraint needs to be acknowledged and appreciated because all I really want to do is take the key back and chuck it at his stupid face.

"Watch the attitude, babe," he warns. "Your thirty seconds are up."

8

He steps away from me and, for the first time since he got in my space, I feel like I can breathe. His scent is intoxicating. He smells of pine, fresh-cut wood, and a bonfire all wrapped up in one.

"Hey, Jackson, it's Warner. Can you send a car out to the cabin? I got a situation," he says into the phone.

My mouth drops open for the second time in ten minutes.

Did he seriously call the cops on me?

"Are you serious right now?" I asked, dumbfounded at how this was happening.

"Alright, thanks." He hangs up the phone. "Cops are twenty minutes out."

"You have lost your fucking mind."

"I've lost my fucking mind? You're the crazy lady breaking and entering."

"Oh, you can not be believed." I'm seething at this point.

"You can wait outside."

"And you can kiss my ass."

That's the last thing I say to him before I park my ass in an old rocking chair behind me that is tucked away in the corner to wait for the cops.

True to his word, red and blue lights flash as they pull into the driveway twenty minutes later.

"Let's go," he orders, trying to rush me out the door.

"I don't think so. I'll talk to him in here, thanks," I reply as I cross my arms and meet his stare, the chair squeaking with each rock.

I'd rather not freeze my ass off while proving that I'm right to this dickwad.

Why are all the hot guys dicks?

Is that a requirement to look like you could throw me over your shoulder and have your way with me?

"Sorry to call you out here so late, Jackson, but she's not leaving, and I'm not in the mood to deal with her myself."

"It's no skin off my nose, Warner. It's what I'm paid to do," the cop, whose name I'm assuming is Jackson, says as he scrapes his boots on the floor mat. "Evening, ma'am. I hear that you're trespassing."

It's not a question, and that pisses me off.

"Well, Officer Jackson, I'm actually not trespassing. I rented this cabin for two weeks. Unlike him." I pause, shooting the grumpy lumberjack a glare. "I didn't break in. I had a key."

"Is that right, Warner?" Officer Jackson's attention moves to him.

"She had a key, but I don't know how she got it," he reluctantly admits.

"I got it because I rented this place online. The listing told me where to find it. If you had listened to me instead of being a fucking jerk, I would have explained that, and we could have avoided all of this mess."

"What listing?" he asks as he stops pacing to stare at me.

"The one you posted online…" I trail off. Because what does he mean, what listing? There's only so many ways I can explain this.

"Oh, fuck." He throws his head back and rubs a hand down his face. "I changed my mind about coming up for Christmas and forgot to take the listing down."

It's hard to keep the smug expression off my face because I knew he was wrong.

"Well, it looks like that's settled. I'm going to head out. See you Friday night, Warner. Evening, ma'am. Enjoy your stay." Officer Jackson smiles at me as he heads out the door, leaving me alone with him.

The officer is better than me because I would have lost my shit for being called out in the middle of the night for something like this, but is that honestly all he's going to do about this situation?

I'm not staying alone with him.

"So, Warner, looks like you need to find somewhere else to stay for the duration of my visit," I tell him as I stand up.

"I'm not going anywhere. This is my fuckin' place," he says, his tone full of frustration as he's looking at me like I'm crazy. "There's a hotel in town. I know they have rooms available. I'll refund you your money."

Now I'm looking at him like he's crazy.

"Oh, I'm sure the hotel in town has rooms available because it looks like it's run by crackheads. Sorry, buddy, but unlike the women you're clearly used to, I do have standards. Do I look like the type of girl who would stay in a place like that?"

His deadpan stare and silence tells me everything I need to know.

The place is infested with roaches.

I don't mean to sound like a stuck-up bitch, but come on. I just drove for around 12 hours because of the stupid snow. I'm not in designer, but I'm also not in shit clothes either. I'm sure my makeup looks horrible by now, but there's no way he isn't getting the picture.

"Goddamnit." He throws his head back again, his hands going to his hips as he lets out a growly sigh that sends a shiver down my spine.

I watch the tendons in his neck bulge out slightly as he swallows. My gaze trails down the rest of him. He has to be at least 6'4 because he towered over my 5'7 frame.

He's not the type I usually go for, but I have to say it was nice to have to look up to someone for a change. Usually, I'm paranoid I'm going to look like a giant towering over my boyfriend because I wore three-inch heels.

This man has me questioning what type of men I've been wasting my time with. Do they all look like this in Michigan?

"You can take my bed. I'll take the couch. You can head out in the morning," he says reluctantly, sounding about as thrilled as he looks.

"I'm not going to take your bed. There isn't a guest room here?" I ask as I really look around for the first time since I walked in.

The floor plan is open, with windows spanning the entire wall the front door is on, offering little privacy, but what I'm sure is an amazing view in the daytime. The kitchen is straight ahead, taking up the back area of the first floor. It's a basic kitchen that needs to be updated. Decades have passed since his fridge and stove were upgraded. They remind me of the ones that were around in the 1950s. It looks like there's a glass door off the kitchen that leads outside.

The living room that we're standing in feels massive with the open floor plan. There's a sectional couch surrounding a stone fireplace that currently has a fire going, the coals burning a bright orange. A giant fur rug spans the area between the sectional and the fireplace, covering the deep oak wood floor.

There's a small dining table big enough to sit four shoved up against the wall opposite the living area, next to where I was sitting in the rocking chair that is also shoved in a corner.

Deer heads decorate the space on the walls that isn't taken up by a window. I feel like I have a million eyes staring back at me, watching my every move.

Basically, you can tell a man decorated this place.

Looking up, I see the stairs leading up to a loft.

A loft with only one bed.

Oh fuck.

I really should have looked at the pictures of the interior before I booked.

"I see it's all starting to click," he says as he crosses his arms, making his pecs bulge out. "Did you not look at the listing before you booked, princess?"

Princess?

"Listen, Warner—"

"It's Logan," he interrupts.

"What?"

"My first name is Logan."

Of course, he would have a hot guy name.

"I'll take the couch, and we can figure this out in the morning," I tell him, my tone final. We aren't getting anywhere tonight and, honestly, I can feel my mood heading further south the longer we talk.

I don't think I've ever met someone who aggravates me this soon into meeting them.

"As much as I've loved meeting you," he pauses as I shoot him a glare because of the sarcasm that's dripping in his tone, "my mama didn't raise me in a barn. You're taking the bed."

Didn't raise him in a barn?

What the fuck does that even mean?

Do they do that up here?

Before I can respond, Logan grabs my suitcase and carries it upstairs without a backward glance. I have no choice but to follow because I don't trust his broody ass not to snoop through my stuff.

I didn't realize truly how high the ceilings were in this place until I'm standing in the loft, looking down at the living space below. I feel like I'm twenty feet up in the air.

"Bathroom is through that door." Logan points to the open door on the other side of the room. "I'll be downstairs if you need anything. Try your best not to, though. I've got shit to do in the morning and need to sleep."

Once again, Logan is jogging down the stairs without so much as an acknowledgment from me.

Figuring that's all I'm going to get for the night, I unzip my suitcase, making sure to let the top hit the wood floor with a bang because fuck him.

This may be his place, but I paid to stay here. I have just as much of a right to be here as he does. Even if it is only for a short time.

Grabbing my toiletry bag and a black silk camisole with matching pants, I head to the bathroom to shower off the day.

I take an extra hot shower that lasts ten minutes longer than it needs to for just rinsing off my body. If he's hellbent on being a jerk, then I'm going to be hellbent on making his life as inconvenient as possible.

Once I'm done and dressed, I exit the bathroom, tossing my toiletry bag back into my suitcase. I'm tempted to peek over the railing just to see what he looks like sleeping, but something tells me he isn't out yet, and I refuse to give in to temptation with a big fat jerk.

Slipping into his bed, the sheets are still slightly warm from when I woke him up. The scent of him covers his pillow; it's the same scent I noticed when he snatched the key from my hand.

Sleep quickly consumes me, but that's expected when you're thinking about being wrapped up in the arms of a man who smells like the bed you're in.

CHAPTER
Three

WYNN

T hud, thud, thud.

My eyes reluctantly open.

What the fuck is that?

My body knows it shouldn't be awake right now. The loft is dimly lit, the only light source coming from the large windows downstairs, and even then it's not that bright, telling me it's still the ass crack of dawn.

Thud, thud, thud.

I let out a low moan as I roll over and bury my face in the pillow.

Why is the noise not stopping?

Pulling the covers over my head, I burrow in, trying my best to go back to sleep. Just as I'm fading in and out, the noise starts up again.

Thud, thud, thud.

"Alright, what the fuck is going on?" I say out loud as I throw the covers off of me. I'm already annoyed, and I'm only on day one of vacation.

Running down the stairs, my silk pants flowing around my ankles, I march to the windows that surround the fireplace and stop dead in my tracks.

My line of sight is zeroed in on a burly man chopping wood with an ax in a flannel and blue jeans that mold to his thighs in a

14

way that looks like they were made for him. His thigh muscles flex with every swing of the ax. His biceps are threatening to rip out of the flannel shirt.

Jesus fucking Christ.

I stand there, unable to move because I'm too zoned in on watching him chop wood like he's some mountain man.

A mountain man who rudely woke me up.

Without thinking, I bang my fist on the window until he stops what he's doing and looks at me.

I throw my hands up in the air and mouth, "What the fuck?"

"What?" he yells back, sounding muffled through the glass.

"What are you doing?" I yell just as loudly.

He cups his ear with one hand, letting me know he didn't hear a word I just said.

Ugh.

Marching to the front door, I slip on my shoes before yanking it open and stepping out onto the massive front porch.

"What are you doing?" I yell again, sounding more annoyed than I did when I asked the first time.

The wintry morning air bites at my arms, tiny shards of ice against my skin. I should have put on a jacket. I cross my arms, rubbing them with my hands, trying to hold onto what little warmth I can. We're locked in a stare-down, and I refuse to be the one who gives in first.

"What are you doing?" I ask for the last time before I grab a ball of snow and chuck it at his face.

"What does it look like? I'm chopping wood." His eyes move to my chest, which is being pushed up by my arms.

Fuck.

I forgot I'm not wearing a bra. My nipples are hard from the cold, and the silky material makes them stand out that much more.

I'm not going to lie; it feels good to know I have the same effect on him that he has on me.

"Now?!"

"It's 8 a.m., princess. Not all of us lie in bed all day. We have shit to do," he says, picking his ax back up and lining it up with another log, dismissing me.

My mouth drops open in shock as I wonder where this man

continues to find his audacity.

God, it's cold out here.

Screw this.

Determined not to let him ruin my vacation, I head back inside to get ready for the day since I'm obviously not going to sleep in around here.

Giving myself one last spritz of perfume, I set the bottle down on the bathroom counter and look in the mirror, trying to give myself a once over but it's nearly impossible because the mirror is the size of a medicine cabinet.

I haven't snooped too much, but from my quick glances, I think this is the only one in the house.

Not that he needs to check himself out because apparently, he's one of the chosen ones who wakes up and looks hot as fuck.

I didn't need to research Michigan winters to know that it was going to be cold. This led me to basically buying a whole new wardrobe for my stay because it doesn't get this cold where I live, and the humidity always makes it feel warmer than it actually is. I'm pretty sure Michigan doesn't know what humidity is. My hair loves it, I will say that. Normally, I'm running a flat iron through it a million times trying to get the frizz out, but it only took a couple pass throughs this morning.

The emerald green sweater I put on makes my raven hair pop. The V is just deep enough to show a hint of cleavage but not enough to give him a show like I unintentionally did this morning. Pairing it with jeans and some black boots, I'm ready to rock and roll.

First thing on my agenda is to make this place look like Santa threw up in here before he holds true to his word of kicking me out. It's what my mom would have wanted.

I still hear the thuds echoing throughout the cabin from him, still cutting wood an hour later as I jog down the stairs with my car keys in hand.

How much wood does one person need?

Logan doesn't even look my way as I head to my car to get the rest of my bags out of the trunk. Not a single word as I make the most unattractive grunts as I haul them through the snow and up the steps of the deck.

"Thanks for the help," I mumble under my breath as I slam the front door closed, hoping he heard the attitude behind the force.

I sigh as I place my hands on my hips and look around the room. He doesn't have a tree up, so that needs to be fixed as soon as possible. Except for a small, old, dusty gas lantern that looks unused, nothing decorates the mantel.

I could decorate the deer. That would be cute.

I can at least start with that and then head into town at the place I found online to find a tree. I wish I could get a massive one because with ceilings like this, you could get a gorgeous tree. But I have no way of getting one of that size back here, though. It needs to be small enough so I can strap it to the top of my car.

Flipping open one of my suitcases, I pull out the prelit garland. The tips of the fake pine needles are dusted with white, like a delicate layer of snow, and little pine cones and berries are tucked throughout. It's perfectly in tune with the cozy vibe of this place.

But first, stockings.

I found the cutest hooks. There's a plaque on the top of each one that will stand up above the garland with the word ho on it. It came in a pack of three, so when read out loud it says, "Ho, ho, ho."

Cute, right?

Christmas was always my mom's holiday that I was just along for the ride with, but once I got in the groove of online shopping, I discovered I have an obsession with gnomes. They're just so fucking cute. Every single one makes me either smile or laugh. I died laughing when I found gnome stockings with actual hair on them to resemble beards, so that's what I bought.

The only thing missing is Christmas music, but I'm going to go out on a limb and say he doesn't have a sound system hooked up here.

I place the stocking holders where I want them, spreading them out on the mantel so they don't look too close together, leaving the rest of the mantel looking bare before I place the garland around it.

Logan comes in from outside as I'm mid-stocking hanging. I don't bother turning around and acknowledging him because he didn't do the same for me. Immature, I know, but I'm not the type to put on a fake personality, Christmas or not. I match energy, and that's what I'm going to do.

"Why does my mantel say 'ho?'" Logan asks from behind me.

Turning around with the last stocking in my hand, I shoot him a glare. "It doesn't say 'ho.' It says 'ho, ho, ho.' Like Santa."

"Sorry, princess, but the way you have it spread out and the garland in between, it doesn't read as 'ho, ho, ho,'" he says, a smirk toying on his lips, the whiskers on his mustache rising with it.

Huh, I think this is the first time I've seen him smile. It looks good on him.

With the last stocking still in hand, I turn back to my work and take a few steps back to examine it.

Goddamnit.

He's right.

"Ugh. I had this all planned out in my mind. I thought it was going to look so cute," I mumble to myself.

"It's something alright. You sure you don't want to go stay at the place in town? I bet you'd fit right in."

My eyes widen as I whip around, coming face to face with Logan, who is trying to contain his laughter but failing miserably.

Is he messing with me?

"Is this funny to you?" I ask, ready to throw this stocking at his face. "Maybe I will go stay there. I bet the crackheads would appreciate my decorations more than you."

"It's a little funny," he says, his laughter dying down. "But about that. I called to see if they had a room, and they don't. They're all booked up. So, I thought about it this morning, and I'm going to refund you your money but still let you stay here. Consider it my apology for the mix-up."

He's still going to let me stay here?

Who is this man, and what happened to the grumpy asshole I met not even twenty-four hours ago?

"But there's only one bed. I also can't let you refund me. It wouldn't be right."

"I'll take the couch. It's big and comfy. Didn't bother me last night. We can agree to disagree about the money. You planning on decorating the whole place?" he asks as he looks around.

"So you're not kicking me out?" I ask just to clarify.

As much as I'm not on board with staying with a random man, I also don't exactly want to turn around and make the long drive back. Plus, what would I do? Text my friends and be like, 'Hey, I'm accepting your invitation after all?'

No, thank you.

I'd rather have the cops called on me again than accept another pity invite.

"Nope." He pops his lips. "Couldn't do it in good conscience with Christmas coming up and all."

"How hospitable of you." I roll my eyes, turning back to the mantel to hang the last gnome stocking up.

"You didn't answer me. You planning on decorating the whole place?" he asks again.

"Yeah," I reply like it's obvious. Who decorates only a mantel? "I'm finishing up this and then I'm going to head into town to get a tree."

There's a long moment of silence. So long that it has me turning back around to face him only to find him looking at me with a you can't be serious expression.

"You're going to get a tree?"

"That's what I just said."

"Have you looked outside?" His facial expression hasn't changed.

I make a show of turning my body to look out the window and looking back at Logan. "Yeah, there's snow. That's kind of the point."

"You got here late last night in the middle of a snowstorm," he says slowly. "How you made it here in that little fucking car is beyond me, but it didn't stop snowing until just before you decided to wake up. The road hasn't been plowed yet. Sorry, but you aren't going anywhere, princess."

My head rears back. "I decided to wake up? You fucking woke me up!"

I don't miss his stupid smirk. "My bad. I didn't realize I was being so loud. Hope you can find it in you to forgive me."

The glare I'm shooting him doesn't do my annoyance justice.

"I'm still getting a tree," I tell him as I turn back to the mantel to look over my handiwork so far.

"You got decorations for it?"

I make a show of walking over to the other two closed suitcases and unzipping them, letting both tops bang against the wood floor to reveal everything else I brought.

"Jesus fucking Christ," Logan says, his eyes widening. "Did you buy out the entire store?"

"No," I say with an eye roll. He thinks an entire Christmas store would fit in two suitcases? "Only about a quarter of it is new. The rest was my mom's. I have another bag of gifts in the backseat of my car that I still need to grab, but that should do it. Unless I make it into town and find more stuff."

"Why aren't you spending Christmas with your mom?"

My mouth opens and closes as I try to figure out what to say. I wasn't expecting him to ask that. If anything, I thought he would make an asshole remark.

The air in the room feels heavy.

I can't tell if it only feels like that because his question cut deep, the sadness I've been trying to block out leaking in, or if it's just from the general shock of it.

Out of the corner of my eye, I catch a glimpse of the ornament my mom used to always hang on the tree last. When it was time, she would make me grab the other side of the ribbon loop so we hung it on the tree together, front and center. The ornament was two snowmen, one an adult and one a child. Mom wrote our names, Wynn and hers, under each snowman. It's cheesy and nothing crazy or unique, but she loved it.

Reaching out my hand, I grab the ornament, pulling it out of the pile.

"No. She, um... isn't around anymore," I tell him as I softly stroke her snowman, each word quieter than the last.

Logan doesn't say anything for a long moment until he decides to break the sad silence. "Grab your coat, princess. I'll meet you outside."

My head shoots up as I look from the ornament to him. "What?" I ask to his back that's halfway out the door.

He doesn't answer me before the front door slams shut.

What just happened?

CHAPTER
Four

WYNN

Logan leaves me staring at the door for all of three seconds before I'm running upstairs, grabbing my coat I had gently laid on my suitcase and meeting him outside.

"That's the coat you brought?" Logan asks in disbelief as he does a double take.

"What's wrong with it?" I ask as I hold my arms out with both hands in the pockets as I look down at myself.

The coat is black fur. Faux fur, of course. I wouldn't be able to live with myself if I knew animals died so I could have a coat. It stops just below my knee and has a collar that goes down to my boobs before it fades into the rest of the coat.

When I saw it online, I thought it was cute and perfect for this trip. It looked cozy and warm, which I figured I would need since it's cold as fuck here. I think my nipples could still cut glass, even in this.

Logan is still looking me up and down, his mouth tipping up in a smile that makes me feel like I'm missing the joke.

"There's nothing wrong with it, princess. Let's go." Logan grabs the handsaw that's resting up against the tire of his older black F-250 and tucks a pair of light brown work gloves in his back pocket, making my eyes land on his ass.

He has on the same red and black flannel he was wearing when he was cutting wood this morning and another pair of blue jeans that look like they were made for him. His flannel is on the thicker side, but not thick enough for me to think it's warm enough for this type of weather.

"Where are we going?" I ask as I trail behind him, trying to keep up as I trek through the snow.

I probably look ridiculous, lifting my legs like I'm doing high-knee drills, because the snow is so deep.

"To get a tree."

"In the woods?"

"Where do you think the trees, like the ones you were going to go look at in town, come from?"

I stop walking as I think about it for a second because, honestly, I feel like a fucking idiot for not having thought of it before.

"Well, I don't know!" I exclaim, throwing my hands up in the air as I realize he didn't stop walking and now I'm struggling to catch up. "Are we cutting this down ourselves?"

I didn't think people actually did that. I thought it was only in the movies. Where I'm from, everyone either has a fake tree they take out of a box every year or they go to the closest hardware store and pick a pre-cut one from the lot.

I think I've unknowingly stepped into a real-life lumberjack land.

"That's what this is for." Logan holds the handsaw in the air and shakes it without faltering a step.

Logan slows down as he looks around, giving me enough time to catch up to him before he abruptly stops, causing me to walk right into his back.

"Oof," I mumble as I hit the brick wall known as Logan's back.

Logan isn't fazed in the slightest. "Take your pick, princess. All of these in this area will fit in the cabin." He waves the handsaw around in a circle, using it as a pointer to show me the area he's talking about.

My gaze follows his hand as I take in all the trees. Some are more of a bright green, while others are more of a blue-green. Some pine trees have needles that are longer and thinner, giving them an almost floppy look, while others have shorter needles that stick more upright, looking thicker.

"I noticed some of your ornaments look a little heavy, so I think your best bet is one that looks like this." He points to the one with thicker needles that has more of a blue tint. "The branches will hold up the weight better, and everything won't sag."

I nod along, acting like I know what he's talking about, when in reality I have no idea. I've always had a fake tree. If an ornament was too heavy, I would just fold the branch in half, and that would hold it.

I walk around a few until I find one that doesn't have any gaps and no branches in it.

"I think this is the one," I say, smiling to myself as I look up at it.

It's taller than Logan by at least a foot.

"You would pick the one that's at least eight feet tall," he grumbles.

Turning to face him, I'm ready to tell him never mind and I can pick a smaller tree, but then I see the smirk on his face as he kneels in the snow, partly climbing under the tree to reach the trunk and know he's just messing with me.

Gone is the asshole I met last night, and in its place is a gorgeous, sarcastic man. I can work with this.

"Do you need help?" I ask, feeling useless as I watch his flannel jacket bunch around the muscles in his shoulders and back as he saws through the trunk.

"Just step out of the way. I don't need a tree falling on you and you ending up getting hurt. The last thing I want to do is spend the night in the emergency room."

I can't help but roll my eyes because how thoughtful of him.

Tucking my hands further into my coat pockets and pulling it tighter against me, I step back. I look up at the tree swaying with each cut. I'm in awe as I watch Logan saw through the trunk with ease. He didn't even grunt. A shiver runs through me, and it's not from the cold. It's from this man, who has gone head-to-head with me from the moment I met him, and I like it. I like that he doesn't cower and give in.

Part of me wishes it were warmer, so I could see him cutting it down without a shirt on.

"Are you sure you don't need any help?" I stupidly ask again, feeling dumb standing around while I watch him cut down a literal fucking tree and too awkward to carry on any sort of conversation.

"No, princess," he grunts. "Just stand there and look pretty in your fur coat."

A slow smirk spreads across my face, aimed right at his back at his admission. I knew he liked this coat.

It isn't much longer before a crack echoes throughout the woods and the tree falls to the ground with a thump, sending snow flying in every direction.

A scream leaves my lips as my arms cover my face on instinct.

"You're okay?" Logan asks as he gently pulls my arms away from my face. "Sorry, forgot to warn you about the snow."

His blue-gray eyes have me locked in a trance. They're warm, matching the rosy pink from the cold on his tan cheeks and nose.

His eyes are dancing around my face as a smile matching mine takes over. I can't do anything but stare. And because of that, I missed his snow-covered glove coming up to my face and tapping the tip of my nose. The light layer of snow transferring to my nose.

I let out a squeal as I jump away, the cold sending a shudder through my body. It doesn't last long before the snow melts and I feel tiny water droplets dripping off.

"I can't believe you just did that." I laugh in shock as I shove his shoulder.

"A little snow isn't going to hurt you." Logan smiles. "Let's get this tree up to the house."

I look around, noting he didn't bring a wagon of any kind.

"You're just going to drag it up to the cabin?" I ask in disbelief.

He's a large man, but I don't see this working out the way he thinks it's going to.

"Yup."

"This might come as a shock, but I can't offer my help on this. I can barely do one 'girl' push-up before my arms start hurting. You're on your own, big guy."

Logan rolls his eyes as he walks over to the tree and grabs the base. "I got it."

Okay, then.

This time, I walk next to him while he drags the tree up to the house. Apparently, that's what it takes to slow him down to my pace.

"Did you bring a stand with you?" Logan asks, breaking the silence.

"What?"

"A stand. Did you bring one?"

"What kind of stand?" I ask, unsure of where he's going with this.

Logan abruptly stops walking and stares at me. "The kind this tree has to go in."

Oh.

Fuck.

"I kind of thought they came with one…" I trail off, unable to look him in the eye.

"You thought they came with one," he repeats slowly.

"The one I bought online for my apartment a few years ago came with one!" I exclaim, throwing my hands up in the air.

I definitely haven't thought this all through.

"Jesus fucking Christ. I see you came real prepared." Logan lets out a loud breath that sounds like he's trying to cover up a laugh. "I probably have one lying around collecting dust in the barn somewhere."

"I came prepared with what matters," I snap.

"Yeah? How were you going to hang all of your ornaments if you couldn't even put the damn tree up?"

"I don't need this kind of negativity ruining my Christmas spirit right now." I sniff as I walk back up to the house, leaving him to drag the tree the rest of the way up by himself.

Logan didn't follow me into the house, and honestly, I'm happy he didn't. It's obvious I'm not familiar with this type of stuff, and I have no idea what I'm doing. I don't need his smart-ass remarks rubbing it in.

I get it's probably a little comical to see someone not know what the fuck they're doing when you've been doing it your whole life, but damn, does it piss me off. I don't know how a man I just met knows how to push every single little button this quickly.

And he enjoys it.

The jerk.

There's only room for one person like that in a relationship, and that's my spot.

After taking my boots off and taking my fur coat back upstairs to its resting spot, I make my way to his kitchen, my stomach grumbling the entire time.

I haven't eaten since I stopped for lunch yesterday, and stupid me didn't even think about hitting up a grocery store on my way through town. I assumed I would have been able to go out sometime today and get what I needed. Getting snowed in didn't cross my mind once.

A loud grunt escapes my lips as I heave open the door to the refrigerator. I'm surprised the handle didn't pop off the way it snapped back.

I didn't know they still sold fridges like this, but going by how Logan is, it was probably here when he bought the place. He hasn't exactly renovated anything.

Hopefully, he doesn't mind me stealing some of his food. I'll replace it the minute the roads are clear and I can leave this place, of course.

He has to eat too, right?

I wasn't up when he woke up, but that was at an ungodly hour, and it's almost three in the afternoon. The only other time he's come inside was when I was decorating the mantel.

I let out a long sigh as I look through his fridge.

There isn't much. In fact, it's practically empty. The drawers that should have fruits and veggies in them are full of bottled water and Natural Light. There's a carton of eggs on the top shelf with a block of cheddar cheese sitting next to it. The shelf below that has something wrapped in butcher paper, which is hopefully going to be my saving grace if it isn't bad.

I pull it out and set it on the counter, and I tear the tape and unwrap the paper to reveal two thick ribeye steaks that look like he bought them not too long ago.

Thank fucking god.

Searching through the rest of the cabinets, I find a few potatoes and mismatched plates and glasses.

Steak and potatoes, it is.

Logan still hasn't come inside by the time I'm heating the cast iron pan for the steaks.

The fire in the living room has long since gone out, leaving a chill in the air, making it so I can't get warm, even with my sweater still on and the oven going.

It took me a solid thirty minutes and a Google search to figure out how to get the oven and stove going. I had to light it with a match.

I couldn't believe it.

Never in my life have I seen an appliance this old still working. It's so old I didn't even know how to use it, but I'll be damned if I walk outside and ask him for help. I refuse to give him anymore satisfaction for the day.

Just as I'm placing the steaks in the pan, the door to the cabin opens, sending a blast of even colder air rushing right past me. My bones feel cold at this point.

"Smells good," Logan says, attitude gone as he shuts the door behind him before hanging his coat up on the single hook nailed into the wall next to the door. "Found a stand in the garage."

I refuse to move from my only source of heat as I turn to look at him. He looks just as good as when I left him, not a hair out of place.

"It's nothing fancy, but it'll work for what you need." He picks the stand up off the floor and holds it out in front of him to show me. "Where do you want the tree?"

Where do I want the tree?

I didn't know I had a choice in the matter.

"It's your house." I shrug. "Wherever you want it."

I just wanted something to decorate. I didn't really factor in the owner staying with me when I rented the place, but if I were alone, I would put it in the only empty corner of the cabin. The one that's near the fireplace and surrounded by windows. That way, if anyone drove by, they could see the whole thing lit up, and maybe it would bring them a tiny bit of joy that didn't make them feel so alone.

Logan looks around the living room and small dining area. His brow lowers slightly as he thinks it over.

God, he's fucking adorable.

"Well, since you picked the biggest tree out there—" I snort as he looks at me with a brow raised. I did not pick the biggest one out there. Not even close. "I think it would fit best in that corner." Logan points to the exact spot I had envisioned it in.

I swallow the lump that's forming in my throat because how did he know?

"I think that's perfect."

He nods his head as he walks over and sets the stand down in the corner.

"I'll bring the tree in after I clean up. Did you make any for me?"

Make any for him?

He laughs at the confused expression on my face. "Food, princess. Did you make enough for me to eat with you?"

Oh fuck!

Turning back to the steaks that I had forgotten about because he's so damn distracting, I flip them over and say a silent thank you they aren't burnt.

"Obviously." I recover with an eye roll. "It's your food. I hope you don't mind I went digging through your kitchen. I'll replace what I used when I can get into town."

"Don't worry about it. We both have to eat. I'm going to clean up real quick before it's ready," Logan says before jogging up the stairs to the loft to shower.

A tingle starts at the base of my spine and heads south. Suddenly, I'm not so cold anymore.

There's something incredibly hot about Logan showering in the same shower I used hours ago. Even though half the time I want to punch the stupid smirk off his face, I can't stop picturing him naked. Or picturing him lathering himself up with soap and rubbing it all over his toned body and grabbing on to his massive cock and stroking that too.

I know it has to be massive because I saw the outline in his gray sweatpants last night. And I know that man wasn't hard.

Jesus.

I can't imagine it getting even bigger. He would rip me in half.

I hear the shower shut off just as I'm plating the steak and potatoes and setting them down at his dining table.

A few moments later, Logan is jogging back down the stairs in the same sweatpants he was wearing last night and the ones I was just thinking about.

Maybe he is trying to kill me.

I'm going to need to go to therapy after this because there's seriously something wrong with me. He annoys the shit out of me, but all I can think about is what I haven't seen yet.

"Looks good," Logan says as he takes a seat across from me. I grabbed a bottle of water for myself and a Natural Light for him. "Thanks for making dinner."

"You're welcome." I cut into my steak and see it's a perfect medium rare.

"You want a beer?"

My nose wrinkles up. "No. I'm not a beer drinker." Especially not one that tastes like dirty water.

"I'm surprised you didn't find a bottle of wine when you were snooping."

My head shoots up from looking down at my plate to find Logan staring at me expectantly.

"I didn't snoop," I snap. "The only things I looked through were your fridge and a couple of cabinets."

"Right," he draws out.

My eyes narrow, not missing the insinuation in his tone that he doesn't believe me.

"I didn't."

"It's okay if you did." He smirks as he pushes his chair back and gets up, going over to the one cabinet I didn't look in and pulls out a bottle of wine. "You like red?"

"If it's dry."

"That's the only kind I'll touch. My sweet tooth is for a different kind of sweet."

My face flushes, and heat spreads throughout my body as I watch him open the bottle.

I fan my face while his back is turned as I try to get myself to calm down. There's something seriously fucking wrong with me because I'm getting turned on watching him open a bottle of wine.

It's probably just his arms.

Anyone would be attracted to a body like this.

He looks like he would just wrap you up and never let go.

It honestly leaves a lot to be desired, even if he gets on my last nerve.

"Here, princess," he says, handing me a glass of red wine in an actual wine glass.

He has wine glasses but no matching dishes?

A girl before me probably left it from the last time he was here.

Now I'm getting pissed, and I have no reason to. Rationally, I know I don't have any claim to this man.

Bringing the glass to my lips, I take a huge gulp because I seriously need to chill the fuck out.

"Eat up. We still have a big ass tree to put up."

Yeah, a big-ass tree I'd like to shove up your ass for giving me this wine glass, but I guess I'll eat my dinner for now.

CHAPTER
Five

WYNN

W e ate the rest of the dinner in silence, with him ignoring me while I glared at him the entire time.

Childish, I know, but I can't help it.

"You done?" Logan asks, looking at my half-eaten plate.

"Yeah," I answer as I set my wine glass I had been swirling around down to grab both of our plates.

"I got it." Logan moves his plate just out of my reach. "You cooked, I'll clean."

How gentlemanlike of him.

"Why don't you just focus on getting the tree in?" I say, leaning over farther and grabbing his plate.

I need a minute to myself that probably will involve another glass of wine to take the edge off.

Maybe that will stop me from wanting to chuck my plate at his head.

Ha ha.

After topping off my glass, I set it down on the counter so I could do the dishes. Looking around, I drop the dirty plate I'm holding back in the sink.

You have got to be kidding me.

There isn't a fucking dishwasher.

Slapping both of my palms on the edge of the counter, I release a long sigh as I hang my head because, fuck my life.

I should have let Logan do the dishes and then bring the tree in.

Pushing off the counter, I open the door under the sink. I find a giant bottle of dish soap with no rag or scrubber in sight.

How has this man survived this long?

Looking around the near-bare kitchen, I'm at a loss on what to do until I remember seeing extra washcloths in the small linen closet upstairs.

It's not my preferred method of washing dishes but it'll have to do.

"I'm getting a scrub brush as soon as I'm allowed to leave this place," I mumble to myself, adding it to my mental grocery list because fuck this.

Just as I'm finishing up, the door to the cabin slams open with a grunting Logan coming through.

I can't see him though, because his entire body is surrounded by the Christmas tree he's currently trying to wrangle in.

"Do you need any help?" I call out, a small smirk on my face, knowing damn well I'm useless.

"God fucking dammit," Logan growls a growl that has a wave of warmth spreading through my body that is not from the wine. "If one more needle stabs me, this thing is going out back and I'm burning it. You won't be getting a fucking tree."

Picking my glass of wine back up, I take another sip as I try to contain the growing smile on my face.

Logan getting stabbed shouldn't make me as happy as it does.

"If you do that, then we'll just have to cut a new one down tomorrow and repeat this process," I say as I lean up against the counter, watching the show.

"There won't be a tree," Logan grunts.

He has the tree almost halfway through the door now. I'm trying not to laugh because the base is the biggest part, and that's where he's really going to struggle.

I failed.

A loud laugh escapes me. "If you don't cut a new one down, I'll just go out there with the saw and do it myself."

Logan abruptly stops what he's doing and lifts his head up. All I can see is the top of his finger-length brown hair and blue eyes drilling a hole into the spot I'm standing in. I'm sure if I could see his mouth, it would be as tight as his brow right now.

"Absolutely not."

"What do you mean, absolutely not?" I ask, crossing my arms and tilting my head.

"Do you know how to use a handsaw?"

"No, but I'm sure I can figure it out. It didn't look that hard."

Actually, it looked really fucking hard. I'm weak. On the off chance I do go to the gym, curling ten-pound dumbbells is a struggle. Logan made it look easy because each of his biceps is the size of my thigh. The man can probably bench press me.

Logan snorts, calling me on my bluff before he goes back to grunting and pulling, completely ignoring me.

A few more minutes pass, and the tree is inside and on the stand.

"Watch your step," Logan warns as I walk toward the suitcase I left open on the floor that has the decorations. "You step on one of those, and it'll hurt like a bitch."

"Do you have a vacuum?" I ask as I look around at the mess. Pine needles are everywhere.

Logan looks up from where he's crouched on the floor, screwing the screws into the tree, giving me a deadpan expression.

"I'm going to take that as a no. What about a broom?"

"There should be one in the back hallway."

Finally, we're getting somewhere.

By the time I have all the needles swept up, Logan has the tree fully secured in the stand.

"Is it time?" I ask, clapping my hands. I can't help but smile brightly at the tree because all I can think about is how happy my mom would be right now.

The only thing missing is the corny Christmas music she would have blasting on repeat and hot chocolate I always refused to drink because it tasted like thick paste going down my throat.

She would pour me a cup anyway, saying that no one likes to drink alone.

"Have at 'er." Logan waves a hand toward the tree as he takes his gloves off. "I'm done fucking with that thing. If it falls over, that's where it's staying."

Running to my suitcase of decorations, I pull out the boxes of light strands I bought. Clear white that does not blink because anything that blinks looks tacky to me. Same with the colored lights.

No one needs every single color on the color wheel on their tree. It hurts my eyes.

"Is that all you got?" Logan asks, making me pause mid sit up with my arms full of small boxes.

I look down at the lights and back up at Logan because I just know he's about to piss me off. "Yeah... why?"

Logan makes a show of looking at the tree. "Because I don't know if it's clicked in your brain yet, princess, but the tree you picked out is fucking huge. Three boxes of lights aren't going to cut it."

I scowl at him. "I'll make it work."

"Suit yourself." He shrugs.

Long story short, Logan was right.

I hate that he's right.

The stupid smirk on his face says it all. I can tell he wants to tell me he told me so, so bad.

The lights look like shit.

"I don't think I've ever seen a tree so poorly lit before, but you somehow managed to nail it." Logan snickers as he cracks open another beer.

"Keep drinking your piss water and keep the commentary to yourself." I sniff. "It doesn't look that bad."

It does.

It looks really fucking bad.

But I'm not going to tell him that.

"I topped off your wine. I'm going outside to get some wood to start this fire. Maybe when I come back in, it'll look better."

"Maybe when I come back in it'll look better," I mock to myself. "Maybe when you come back in you can kiss my ass."

"Maybe I will," Logan says over his shoulder before the front door slams closed, making my eyes widen.

Fuck.

I didn't think he would hear that.

Looking over at the end table Logan has next to his couch, I see my wine glass that he set there for me, and I can't help but

34

smile a little.

It's like he knows when to push and pull with me. How that can happen with someone I met not even twenty-four hours ago is beyond me. My best friends, whom I've known for a decade, don't even get me on this level. Usually, they piss me off, but they don't know they've pissed me off, and that makes me more pissed.

It's a vicious cycle, really.

I spent the next thirty minutes strategically placing the ornaments. I try to disguise that I don't have enough lights to cover the whole tree. There's a solid six-inch gap between each strand staring back at me.

I definitely did not bring enough ornaments to cover this thing.

Just as I'm placing the last ornament I have—the snowmen of my mom and me—Logan comes back inside with his arms full of wood.

"Let me guess, that's all the ornaments you brought, eh?"

"Yes," I answer, gritting my teeth as I pick up the bronze tree topper.

Looking at the topper and up at the top of the tree, I'm wondering how in the hell I'm going to get this one. The tree is well over two feet taller than I am.

"Need help with that?" Logan asks as he stacks the wood he brought in next to the fireplace.

"I can manage," I sass, not wanting to hear anymore remarks out of him.

"It doesn't look like you can manage, princess. You think you're going to magically grow a few feet?"

My shoulders slump as I sigh.

I'm beginning to hate how he's always right.

"Do you have a ladder I can use?" I ask.

"Don't need one."

Turning to face Logan, I ask, "What do you mean I don't need one?"

I barely get my question out before Logan is crouching down in front of me. "Climb up."

Um… What?

"Climb onto what?" I ask stupidly.

"Me." He taps the back of my calf.

35

I try to step back, but his large hand locks on my calf, holding me in place. My body is on fire as if he's touching me everywhere when really it's only one spot. All I can think about is what his rough hand would feel like rubbing all over me.

"I'm not going to say it again. Climb up."

"Yes, sir." I salute without thinking about what I just said.

Sweet baby Jesus, did I really just call him sir?

"I like that," Logan rumbles.

Figuring it's best to keep my mouth shut because I can't be trusted with what comes out of it, I pick the only option that's left. I climb the fuck on.

I swing one leg over the right side of his shoulder before using his head to steady me as I swing the other leg over.

Holy shit, his hair is soft.

I can't stop myself from running my fingers through it, lightly scratching his head with my nails as I go. The brown locks are long enough to grab on to and look the hot type of messy I love, but short enough not to look unkempt. It's the perfect length.

"Mmm… that feels good," Logan rumbles again, this time leaning into it.

The rumble rakes through his whole body, vibrating my core. I don't think I've ever experienced something so erotic when all my clothes are on.

I wiggle slightly on his shoulders, willing to do anything to relieve some of the ache that's building.

His hand that was holding my calf has worked its way up my leg and is now digging into my upper thigh, holding me in place.

"Not too much of that. I didn't get dessert, and you smell delicious, princess."

I clear my throat as I snap out of the Logan fog he sucked me into.

Thank God he can't see my face because I would die from embarrassment. I was practically grinding my vagina on his neck.

Who in the hell does that?

"Let's get the star on the tree," I say, powering through as I ignore him when really all I want to do is take him up on his offer.

If it even is an actual offer.

Without a word, Logan stands up effortlessly with me on his

shoulders as I accidentally pull his hair to keep from falling off at the abrupt movement.

"I'm so sorry," I rush out.

God, can this get any worse?

"Don't apologize for something I like you doing."

Even with being on his shoulders, I still have to lean over and stretch my arm out as far as it will go to reach the top, forcing his head to nestle in between my breasts.

I quickly place the star on top of the tree and move my chest back slightly. I hold my breath as I wait for him to say something as he lowers back down, but he doesn't. Releasing his hair, I climb off of him.

"Thanks for your help," I tell him as I step back, because what else am I supposed to say?

Thanks for the ride?

I don't fucking think so.

Deciding I'm done for the day, I plop my ass on the couch to admire my tree and mantel and watch him work. Tucking my feet under my legs, all I can think about is I wish I had brought some blankets.

Logan's bachelor pad doesn't exactly have any throws lying around.

"So what brought you here?" Logan asks as he arranges a few logs in the fireplace.

"I wanted to get away for the holiday and actually experience a white Christmas."

Logan snorts. "You got what you wished for. It's coming down hard out there."

"Again?" I ask, dread filling my tone.

It's official. I'm never leaving this place.

"Yup. If they don't get the road plowed tomorrow, I'll take you into town in Old Red. I've got guys' night with the boys."

Of course, he would name his truck.

I can't roll my eyes hard enough.

"Is that what the officer you called to have me arrested said he would see you on Friday for?"

"I didn't call him to have you arrested." Logan scowls. "I just wanted you gone."

"That's the biggest lie I ever heard." I snort. After a beat of silence, I ask, "Do you still want me gone?"

I hold my breath, unsure of his answer.

I still can't get a good read on him and to be honest, I'm not one hundred percent sure how I feel about him, either.

"No," he answers after a few minutes.

No?

That's it?

"That sounds reassuring." I roll my eyes, but inside I'm dying. I barely know him, but there's this attraction I can't explain that I know I would feel a giant void if I left now. "I can leave as soon as I can get out of here and confidently say I won't end up in a ditch or stuck somewhere."

"I got you a tree, didn't I?"

My heart twinges because, yeah, that's great, but…

"Take it as my apology for being an asshole last night."

My eyes widen as I glance his way. That was not what I was expecting to come out of his mouth.

"I don't think I ever thanked you for cutting down the tree and bringing it in," I whisper as I look into his eyes.

The fire behind him casts a warm glow, making his blue eyes stand out, their intensity almost pulling me in.

"Is that your way of saying you accept my apology?" he asks just as softly.

"Yes," I answer, still whispering.

There's no sense in holding a grudge against him over this. Once Christmas is over, I'll probably never see him again.

"Good."

Clearing my throat, I look away, needing a break from this moment that became intimate way too quickly without either of us realizing it.

It's a good kind of uncomfortable in a way that I've never experienced, and I think that's what makes me feel unsettled with it because how can I have moments like this with a complete stranger?

"So I take it that this is your cabin, obviously," I say as he nods his head as he stokes the fire, giving me this subject change. Logan is sitting on the ground next to the fireplace with his legs cocked, beer in one hand and stoker in the other. I want nothing more than to climb into his lap, but I don't. "Do you come up here every year for Christmas?"

"Only if we're expected to get a lot of snow. I plow a few of the businesses in town."

My brow lowers and my head tilts to the side as I think about what he just said.

"So you're saying that all this time you could have plowed our way into town?" I ask, sounding slightly bewildered.

"It doesn't work like that, princess," Logan says, his eyes dancing as a smile takes over his face. "Once the snow lets up, the county boys will come through and plow the roads. Ours will probably be one of the last because it's not a main road. Then I'll head into town and clear the parking lots that need to be cleared."

"So you come up every time it snows?" That seems a bit much considering I drove over ten hours just to get here myself. "Where do you live when you're not here?"

"A couple of hours south of here."

So, not a bad drive then.

"What do you do for work when there isn't snow?" I don't think I've ever heard of someone snowplowing on the side as their full-time job, but what do I know? Where I'm from, the entire town shuts down on the rare chance they see one tiny snowflake.

Logan lets out a loud laugh, startling me. "You think me plowing a few businesses in the winter is my full-time job? Fuck you're cute."

My face heats from a mixture of embarrassment and his calling me cute.

Mainly the cute part because this is the first real compliment he's given me and a verbal indicator that maybe he's into me aside from him checking me out earlier.

"Well, I don't know!" I exclaim, throwing one hand up in the air because I refuse to risk spilling my wine. "I don't judge what people do for money. Unless it's like murdering people or something, but even then, I think there are exceptions to that." I ramble.

"Are you telling me you're here to kill me?" Logan asks, fighting laughter. "If you are, all I ask is that you do it in that fur coat of yours."

My eyes narrow at him as it takes everything in me to fight my smile. "There's nothing wrong with my fur coat."

"Of course not, princess." Logan's eyes are dancing.

"I'm glad you find this so hilarious. Not all of us look good in flannel."

"So you think I look good." It wasn't a question.

"Um…" I trail off, trying to think of something quick to say because I didn't mean to let that slip out, let alone him pick up on it. "Oh, come on! You know you're attractive. I'm sure you have women hitting on you constantly."

"I don't care if other women think I'm attractive. I care if you do."

Holy shit.

I'm pretty sure my face matches the color of the Cabernet he poured for me. What the fuck is happening?

My mouth opens and closes because once again I'm at a loss for words within a minute. That's what this man does to me. He turns me inside out and in directions I didn't even know existed for me.

Logan shoots me a panty-melting smile before going back to my original question. "I'm a farmer."

My mouth hangs open in shock.

I don't know what I was expecting, but it wasn't that.

Jesus Christ, no wonder he looks so good in jeans and a flannel.

He's probably throwing around hay bales all day long and wrangling animals.

Once again, I find myself eyeing his biceps, which are looking all snug and defined against the material of his shirt.

I bet he could throw me around.

"What do you do?" Logan asks, breaking me from my thoughts.

"What?"

"What do you do?" he repeats, the smirk on his face not going anywhere.

"Oh, I work in HR for a smaller tech sales company. Nothing crazy." I wave my hand, blowing it off.

"It doesn't need to be crazy for you to be passionate about it. Do you like it?" Logan asks, the smirk on his face long gone. A serious one is in its place, like he's hanging on to every word I say and storing it away for future use.

Do I like it?

What a loaded fucking question because at the end of the day no, I hate it actually. My boss doesn't care about anyone as an actual person. We're all just a number to him. Every single day I come home from work, I feel mentally exhausted even if nothing happened that day. Walking into the office has been sucking the life out of me lately.

"I wouldn't say HR is my passion," I admit out loud for the first time.

"So you hate it."

"Pretty much." I sigh, angling myself deeper into the corner of the couch. "But it pays the bills."

"There are a lot of other things out there that pay the bills," Logan says as he studies me.

He's not wrong about that, but only if it were that easy to switch. The job market is crazy where I live, and very rarely is the grass greener on the other side.

"Is farming your passion?" I ask, taking the focus off me.

Logan takes a long swig of his beer, his Adam's apple bobbing with each swallow before answering, "It's all I know. I wouldn't say farming in general is my passion, but hard work that puts food on the table for thousands of other families is."

Since when have I thought that's attractive?

Everything this man does turns me on in the smallest ways I didn't even know were possible.

"Is it a family thing?"

I would think it would have to be. I know people have small hobby farms, but the way Logan talks about it, his sounds massive.

"Third generation. My brothers and I took over a few years ago when my dad decided to retire. He's still bossing us around every chance he gets, though, so I say retired loosely."

"That must be nice." I smile softly.

It was always just my mom and me. There wasn't anything generational about us until now, I guess. I'm trying to carry on her Christmas tradition, but besides that, she ran to the beat of her own drum.

"It is," Logan replied just as softly. "Annoying at times because everyone is in everyone's business, but we all love each other and would do anything for the other."

I have no idea what that would be like. My best friend Cara and I were up in each other shit when we lived together, but she eventually got married and a natural distance was created.

"Well, I think I'm going to turn in for the night," Logan says as he gets up off the floor.

The fire has died down a little, but the coals are still glowing orange. It's taken the chill out of the cabin.

"I'll take the couch tonight. It's only fair we trade."

"You're not sleeping on the couch."

"Logan, be serious right now. I'm here for a while. You're honestly going to sleep on the couch for days on end?" I'm still trying to wrap my head around how a man his size can even fit comfortably on this couch. It's big but still.

"I'll be fine, Wynn. Take the bed or I'll carry you up there myself."

Every fiber of my being wants that. I would be living out every girl's fantasy being carried around by a big strong lumberjack.

That fantasy isn't happening tonight, though.

Instead, I get up from the couch, put my empty wine glass in the sink to hand wash tomorrow, and head upstairs to the loft by myself.

There is a slight chill up here compared to downstairs, but it isn't unbearable. All it does is make me wish I were sliding into bed with Logan while he wraps me up and takes the chill away.

CHAPTER
Six

WYNN

My eyes fly open.

The wood beams on the ceiling are the first thing that greets me.

Thud. Thud. Thud.

You have got to be fucking kidding me.

I thought we had reached a mutual agreement last night that we were putting all of this behind us, but here I am getting woken up at the ass crack of dawn again.

Throwing the covers off of me, I stomp downstairs. This time I'm not in a silk pajama set but in a silk nightie that stops mid-thigh with a deep V that leaves little to the imagination and is clingy in all the right places.

It's a gorgeous moody blue-gray that ironically matches the person's eyes I want to strangle right now. The silk hem is lined with black lace. Needless to say, it's fucking hot.

Once I reach the lower level, I see Logan outside, chopping wood through the window with zero care for the people that are still sleeping.

That person being me.

I continue my trek and stomp over to the door, only pausing to slip my shoes on before yanking open the front door.

"Are you kidding me right now?" I yell, throwing my hands up in the air.

Logan pauses mid-swing as he looks up at me.

His eyes quickly widen before he schools his face, trying to hide his reaction to me as they hungrily roam my body. It was so quick that if I hadn't been looking right at him, I would have missed it.

"What?" Logan asks, like he doesn't know why I'm out here.

"What do you mean, what? We just fucking talked about this!"

Logan stares at my bouncing breasts, their movement mirroring every arm and head movement because I skipped wearing a bra again.

I clear my throat as I place my hands on my hips, drawing the nightie up slightly higher. It's barely touching my thighs at this point.

Goosebumps pepper my skin from the cold morning air, but the feeling doesn't register. All I can feel is the heat in Logan's gaze.

"What?" Logan asks again.

"I swear to God if you say what one more time like you don't know what I'm talking about, I'm going to come over there and shove the ax up your ass," I snap.

"If you come over here, there will be something shoved somewhere, but it won't be my ass."

I'm sorry, what?

Did he just say what I think he said?

"Am I not allowed to sleep in around here?" I ask, it now just hitting me that I'm standing out here with almost everything on display.

"You can sleep in however late you want, princess, but if you want heat, and judging by the way your pretty tits have their attention on me, I think you do, I need to chop some fucking wood."

"You don't have to be so crude about it," I snap, not moving to cover up.

"And you don't have to march out here and tempt me with what I haven't earned the right to touch yet," Logan retorts.

My mouth opens and closes as my ability to form a coherent sentence flies out the window.

In all of my thirty years, no one has ever tried to earn the right to anything with me.

With one last glance, I spin around and stomp back inside to

44

get ready for the day, since I know I won't be able to go back to sleep.

"Love to watch you go almost as much as I love to watch you come, princess," Logan says to my back.

I dare myself to see the smirk on his face that I know is there as I quickly work up the courage to glance over my shoulder, knowing my face is on fire. What I wasn't expecting is the wink he shoots me, sending a shiver down my spine as I shut the door behind me and lean up against it as I try to regain my bearings.

He has a way of knocking me off my axis with one move. I mean, who winks and looks that hot doing it? Usually when a guy winks at me, it gives me the fucking ick. There's just something about a big, burly man holding an ax that does it for me.

As I walk up the stairs to the loft, I swear I can feel Logan's eyes following me through the windows with every step I take.

By the time I'm ready and back downstairs, Logan is plowing the drive. It hasn't snowed yet today. The key word being yet, but I'm still holding out hope today will be the day I finally get to explore in town.

Today I decided to go with a pair of fleece-lined leggings, a low-cut form fitting black tee, and an oversized gray cardigan that makes you want to curl up on the couch with a good book and never leave.

Standing in the middle of the room with my hands on my hips, I look around at what still needs to be done.

The tree skirt still needs to be placed so I can put the presents I brought under it. I have a few various snowman decor items I brought in case there were tables or counters I could decorate as well.

"I guess I'll start with the tree skirt," I mumble to myself as I walk over to the suitcases I left on the floor and pull out the skirt I'm looking for.

It's nothing fancy. I found a black and white checkered print that resembles flannel, but it's not actual flannel when I was shopping back home and thought it was so cute. I figured it would

break some decorations up to keep it from looking too…
Christmasy, if you know what I mean.

There's a fine line, and every year as a kid my mom would
blow right past it until she had bells dangling off of a sweater. I
was always so embarrassed to go anywhere with her dressed like
that, but now I just wish she was still around.

Just as I have the skirt laid out how I want, the front door
opens.

"Oh great. More decorations," Logan says as he comes inside
and takes his boots off.

I narrow my eyes at him. "You thought last night was it?"

"I was hoping it was enough."

"Well, lucky for you I actually wanted to go into town and see
if there are decorations I can get that are on theme."

"On theme?" Logan asks, his brow lowers in confusion.
"Aren't all decorations on theme? It's fucking Christmas."

"You know what I mean," I say with an eye roll.

"No, I really don't, so please explain."

"I want it on theme with Northern Michigan."

"Do we have different stuff from you down south?"

"I don't know. I haven't shopped here before."

"Oh, Jesus Christ." Logan sighs as he rests his forehead on his
hand. "I didn't realize my telling you we can go into town was
going to involve this."

"You're welcome." I smile at him. "Are you ready?"

"Let me shower and change real quick, and then we can head
out. I'm all sweaty."

"I think you look hot, sweaty."

A slow smirk takes over Logan's face.

Fuck.

Did I say that out loud?

"Good to know, princess." Logan winks before jogging
upstairs.

Kill me now.

Logan doesn't leave me waiting for long. I'll forever be
envious of how guys can shower and throw on clothes and call it a
day. It takes all of five minutes to get ready.

If I did that, I would walk out of here looking like a drowned rat.

"Are the roads all plowed?" I ask as I follow him out.

"We're about to find out."

"You think we'll make it if they aren't?" I understand he has a truck, but there's a reason the plow trucks are massive, right? I would imagine even this would get stuck in something.

"Ol' Red will make it, princess. I've been driving her for the last ten years. She hasn't let me down once."

Watch this be the first time she does.

She.

I can't believe I'm referring to his truck as a female now. What is with guys and naming vehicles?

Mine and Logan's hands reach for my door handle at the same time, causing me to step back in reaction.

I don't get far, though, because I smack right into Logan's chest.

"Ope," Logan mumbles, resting the hand that's not on the door handle on my waist. "Just opening the door for you."

"Thank you," I mumble back as he opens the door, not letting me out of his hold.

I bask in it.

His hard, warm body all around me. It feels like he's teasing me because all I've thought about since that first morning is what it would feel like to be wrapped up in his arms with him holding on so tight like he never wants to let me go.

But like everything with Logan so far, the moment is over before it can really begin.

Do I want it to begin?

I guess it wouldn't be the worst thing in the world.

I leave to go back to Virginia in less than two weeks. I would never see him again. It's honestly the perfect no strings attached situation.

I've always been the relationship type of girl, never having so much as a one-night stand in my life, but I can't imagine leaving here without experiencing everything that is Logan just once.

In fact, I want it so badly that I think if I did, it might end up being one of my biggest regrets in life.

Even though I want to punch him in the face ninety percent of the time.

Sliding into the passenger seat, I sink into the seat slightly as I look around in shock.

It's a fucking mess.

I can't even see the floor in the backseat. It's covered with random tools, rags, hats, and coffee cups. You name it, and it's probably in his backseat.

"I know, I know. I need to clean it out," Logan says as he slides into the driver's seat, taking in my wide-eyed expression.

"What happened?"

"It's my work truck." He shrugs. "I don't ever have someone riding in here with me unless it's one of my brothers who needs a ride to where we're at in the fields that day."

"I'm going to take a wild guess and say their trucks probably look the same," I say as I inhale deeply.

The one thing I can get behind is the smell. It smells like oil mixed in with Logan's scent. It smells like a man who works with his hands and knows how to use them.

Logan lets out a loud laugh as he drives. "Good guess."

Even though he plowed the driveway this morning and it hasn't snowed since yesterday, I still can't stop myself from wincing as I hear the crunch of snow as we pull out of the drive and onto the road that's still unplowed.

My hand immediately grabs onto the oh-shit handle for dear life as if that's going to save me.

Logan looks over at me, his expression half amused and half looking like I'm crazy. "What are you doing?"

I can't take my eyes off the road long enough to fully face him, so I spare him a side glance. "Making sure I don't die."

"…and you think holding onto the oh-shit handle is going to save you? Baby, I hate to break it to you, but if we get in a wreck that will kill us, that handle isn't saving you." This time I take my eyes off the road to shoot Logan a glare that is becoming my signature look for him and his smartass remarks. "Your fur coat has a better chance of saving your life. All that fluff acting like a fucking airbag."

Goddamnit.

I can't even say anything smart back. I'm fighting the grin off

48

my face because that was fucking funny.

"The universe steered me in the right direction with buying it then," I sass, turning back to the road, the smile not leaving my face.

"It steered you here, so it must be doing something right."

My head whips back at his admission, but his eyes are on the road, not paying me any attention.

Did he really just say that?

Just as I'm about to ask him what he meant by that, we turn onto the main road.

The plowed main road.

"I don't want to say I told you so, but…"

"Point taken, big guy."

Logan's head swings my way. "Big guy?"

"What? You know you're not small. You're like a big, burly lumberjack who wakes me up early as fuck every single morning and wears the same flannel every day." I shrug. "And don't think I don't know that you chop wood that early on purpose."

I know he's doing it to get a rise out of me. No one wakes up that early because they want to. And if they do, I'm pretty sure they're a serial killer, and I'll probably see them on a new episode of Forensic Files.

"First of all, this is the only flannel I brought with me. For your information, I have two more at home. And second of all, I wake up early because I want to get that shit done. No one in their right mind wants to spend all day chopping wood."

"But does it have to be every morning? It seems a little excessive if I'm being honest."

And annoying.

Very fucking annoying.

"You want heat, don't you?"

I sigh dramatically as I relax slightly in my seat, my head leaning back into the head rest. "I guess so."

"You guess so? I didn't miss the way you were shivering when I came in from hauling the tree up last night."

"Whatever," I mumble, giving in fully to trusting his driving as I let go of the oh-shit handle and cross my arms.

"Is there anywhere you wanted to stop?" Logan asks, breaking the comfortable silence that has settled in the truck.

"No, I didn't really look at what shops were in town when I booked this place online. Is there any knickknack shops or something similar?"

"I have no idea what that means, but I'll take you to the area my mom usually goes to when she comes up."

That reminds me, I've been meaning to ask him about that.

"Why are you up here by yourself for the holiday when all of your family is back home?" I ask, not caring one bit if I'm prying.

"Well, my mom got a wild hair and decided to take her and my dad on a cruise in protest because she doesn't have any grandkids yet. So that left my brothers and me, who are fine doing our own thing."

"So let me get this straight. Your mom, who I'm assuming usually hosts holidays, decided not to host Christmas this year because you haven't given her grandkids?"

Taking away a whole holiday for the whole family seems like such a vindictive way to get what you want.

I kind of fucking like it.

"Me?" Logan's hand leaves the wheel and goes to his chest as he looks at me. "There's a 'we' here. This doesn't all fall on me. I've got three other brothers who are perfectly capable of reproducing. I'm kind of surprised it hasn't happened already."

"Where do you fall in line?"

"I'm the oldest."

I can totally see that.

He's bossy, determined to do what he wants regardless if it bothers someone else, and not to mention stubborn. I've picked up on all of that in just the few days I've known him, so I can only imagine how he is at home on the farm.

"You're what, like thirty-five?" I ask as I look him up and down.

I can't imagine he's older than that. There's some gray hair sprinkled throughout his beard, but it's nothing crazy. It just makes him that much hotter.

He has a few hard lines on his forehead and those cute wrinkles around his eyes, but that's it.

"You think I'm thirty-five? I'm flattered," Logan says, as a wolfish grin spreads across his face. "I'll be 42 in August."

My eyes widen in shock, and my mouth drops open.

"No, you're not."

There is no way this man is forty-two years old. When I guessed thirty-five, I was giving him an extra year or two to be generous.

"Swear on my nana's grave. You can look at my driver's license if you don't believe me."

"Jesus, no wonder your mom wants grandkids. You're basically fifty." I slap my hand over my mouth because I can't believe I just said that.

A loud laugh booms out of Logan, making me jump in my seat.

"Okay, smartass, and how old are you? Twenty-five? Talk to me in another ten years and let me know how you're doing."

"You think I look like I'm twenty-five?" I ask, side-eyeing him as I try to contain my smile because I'm elated.

I've spent an embarrassing amount of money over the last couple of years on various serums, creams and washes that basically claim they will age your skin backwards.

I have yet to see that claim in action.

Logan nods his head yes.

"Now I'm the one who's flattered. I'm thirty. Thirty-one in June."

It's Logan's turn to look at me in shock. "No, you're not."

"Swear on my mom's grave. We can exchange driver's licenses if you want. You should be able to see it on the site you used to rent out the cabin. I had to put it on there to book."

"My mom is the one who handles all of that. I can barely use my phone," Logan admits.

Ah, so he's a mama's boy. I guess that makes sense. From what little he's said about his family, they all seem really close. I mean, they work together, for God's sake. I don't think I could even work with my best friend. I love her to death, but damn, can she get annoying.

"So your mom knew she booked my stay, didn't tell you and still let you come up here?"

Logan's hand runs down his beard as he thinks about it. "Yeah, she sure did. Some mom she is. She could have trapped me with a serial killer for all I know."

"Me?" I ask, my voice rising slightly.

"Yeah, you. Ready to smother me with your fur coat at any chance you get."

Rolling my eyes, I turn my attention to look out the window, watching the buildings in town pass with a smile on my face. "Maybe you should watch it then because each day it's sounding like a better and better idea."

I didn't get to see much of the town when I drove through the first time because it was pitch black out combined with what I'm pretty sure was a blizzard. I was too busy concentrating on not dying.

But this place is gorgeous.

I haven't even stepped out of the truck, and I can already feel the small-town atmosphere spilling in.

It reminds me of a town taken right out of a Hallmark movie with the old brick buildings. Every light pole is decorated with lights going up it and a wreath hanging off it. A few have a small banner hanging off of them advertising a Christmas parade that's happening this weekend.

"Do you actually know every person you're waving to?" I ask as he pulls into a parking spot on the street.

Ever since we got into town, he's waved at at least five people walking past us on the sidewalk.

That doesn't happen where I'm from. In fact, I'd say people go out of their way not to acknowledge someone.

I know I do.

I make a conscious effort to look in the opposite direction or force my eyes to focus on something else that isn't them.

"Some I do, some I don't. It's the polite thing to do." He shrugs.

It's the polite thing to do.

"You just pick and choose your polite then, huh?"

"When have I not been polite to you? I let you stay with me after you broke into my place," Logan says as he puts the truck in park and turns in his seat to face me.

"Um, you waking me up early as fuck," I say sarcastically. "And I did not break into your place. I had a key."

"Semantics." Logan taps my thigh. "Not sure what you're looking for, but all of these shops up and down this street have shopping shit in them. I need to go plow a couple of businesses, but I'll be back for you."

"You don't want to go shopping with me, big guy?" I tease as I unbuckle my seatbelt.

"I want to go shopping with you as much as I want to stab myself in the eye," Logan says, giving me a deadpan look. Ugh, men and their aversion to shopping. "I'll be back."

"Have fun. Thanks for the ride and don't forget about me," I say as I slam the door shut.

I don't know if it was a figment of my imagination, but I could have sworn I heard him say how could I ever forget about you right before the door shut.

CHAPTER
Seven

WYNN

'm so out of place it isn't even funny.

I'll never admit it to Logan, but now I get why he thought the fur coat was so funny.

No one here has one.

In fact, I'm getting looked at like I'm the crazy one.

All the women here are wearing something similar to what Logan wears, just the female version, which, in my opinion, barely looks any different.

"Come on in," a lady calls from the back as I walk into a shop that has Christmas decorations in the window display, the bell chiming loud. It caught my eye and seems promising. "Can I help you find anything?" A short, older lady with a smile on her face emerges behind the register.

I watch her not so subtly look me over. She doesn't say anything, but it's written all over her face.

That seems to be the trend.

"No, I'm just browsing. Thank you, though." I smile as I move further into the store.

"Holler if you need anything," she says before heading back to where she was when I first came in.

"Thanks," I call after her, unsure if she heard me or not.

I brought gifts for myself, which now I'm thinking Logan might find a little weird, but oh well. I wasn't counting on anyone else being here, though, so I have nothing for him. I wonder if I should get him something small so it's not as weird.

What would Logan like?

He's obviously an outdoors type of guy. The problem with that is I am not an outdoors type of girl. Unless you count drinking margs on a patio outside in the summer as being outdoorsy.

I have to turn my body sideways as I round some of the corners of the aisle because this store is jammed packed. Some of it is a little too gaudy for my tastes, but I can see the appeal in this area.

I feel like I have to get Logan another flannel since I gave him shit for wearing the same one, but I'm not going to find that here. This looks to be only household knickknack stuff.

Just as I'm about to head back to the front of the store to leave, a display stand of ornaments catches my eye.

The one that caught my eye is much like the snowman one I have from my mom except this is gnomes in a row with blank spaces underneath, leaving room to write a name. One gnome wears a flannel jacket, and the other has a flannel scarf.

How fucking cute.

If only the other one had a fur coat, but I can just act like it does in my head.

It would be kind of weird to get an ornament like this for Logan with our names on it, wouldn't it?

I mean, we just met, and I wasn't even supposed to meet him. It happened by chance. Holiday ornaments are like years into dating territory, not I'm crashing at your place because your mom fucked up the reservation.

"I can personalize that for you right here if you would like," the lady who greeted me says, making me jump because she scared the shit out of me sneaking up on me like that. "Sorry, dear, I didn't mean to scare you. When you get this old, the only way to move is slow and steady. It's hard to hear me coming."

Turning around with the gnome ornament in hand, I look at her, taking in her gray hair and light makeup. She looks good for her age.

"What are you talking about? You don't look a day over thirty."

She lets out a loud laugh. "I'll take the compliment. So, whose name am I putting on that?"

I look down at the ornament in my hand, at a loss of what to do. "Oh, um… I don't know. I'm not sure if the person will like it."

"Well, how about this? The ornaments are on sale for ten bucks. If they don't like it, you only wasted ten bucks. You can spend that at the gas station nowadays. It's like the new dollar."

She has a point.

Everything is fucking expensive now.

I don't think anyone has ever used it as a sales tactic against me, but I admire the hustle.

"Alright." I shrug. "I'll do it."

The worst thing that can happen is it leaves in my suitcase with me as a memory of this trip.

"Great!" She beams as she takes the ornament out of my hand and walks up to the register. "What are the names?"

I stare at the gnomes as my chest tightens. "Logan and Wynn."

Her eyes raise to me. "Pretty name for a pretty girl."

My chest still feels like it's getting tighter with each breath I take, so all I can muster is a tight smile.

Her hands are shaky as she uncaps the marker, but once she starts writing, the names flow effortlessly.

And they look good together.

God, I feel like that girl in middle school who would write her and her crush of the week's names a million times all over a notebook. Which seems pretty pathetic at my age, but here I am staring at our names together like there may be a small sliver of hope I'll get to see what's underneath those tight jeans Logan is always wearing.

"There." She caps the marker and picks up the ornament, holding it out for me. "What do you think before I wrap it up?"

I gently take it from her, cradling it in my hands as if it's something precious.

"It's perfect. Thank you," I tell her softly.

"Glad you think so. It'll be $10.60 with tax."

I hand over my card as she swipes it and wraps it up in tissue paper.

"Do you happen to know if there is a shop within walking distance from here that sells flannel shirts?"

She looks up from her wrapping, giving me a deadpan expression. "Girl, I can tell from your fur coat that you aren't from around these parts, but this is Northern Michigan. Flannel is sold all year round here. Hit the shop on the corner. They will have everything you need. Even flannel underwear." Her voice gets lower at the end, as if she doesn't want someone to hear her talking about panties even though she and I are the only ones in the store.

"Great, thanks." My tight smile is back as I take my bag from her.

I'm thankful she told me where to go, but I hate when people make me feel like I'm stupid. How am I supposed to know it's sold all year round? It seems like a winter thing to me.

"Oh, and if you're feeling like a little holiday cheer, stop into the place next door. It'll warm you up like that." She winks as she snaps her fingers together.

"I'll keep that in mind," I tell her as I push open the door and step out onto the street.

Curiosity got the best of me as I headed to the shop next door, because what in the world is holiday cheer?

I grab the handle to the front door and pause as I scan the street for any sign of Logan but come up empty.

Stepping in, I take a moment for my eyes to adjust to the dim lighting.

I can't help but let out a short laugh as I take in my surroundings.

She really told me to go to a bar.

It's not busy. There's a couple at one booth and a few people at the rail, but that's it. Deciding I don't want to take up an entire table to myself on the off chance someone comes in that needs it, I take a seat at the bar.

"What can I get for ya?" a middle-aged woman asks as she sets a coaster down in front of me.

"Ah… the lady next door told me to stop in here for some holiday cheer," I tell her, but it comes out sounding more like a question because I just realized how ridiculous that sounds as I say it out loud.

"Good day for it. It's a cold one out there," she says as she turns to the wall of liquor behind her.

She didn't act like she didn't know what it was.

Is this a thing here?

My eyes widen as I watch her grab the Fireball off the shelf and pour a decent amount into a shaker.

Oh no.

I am not a whiskey girl.

If Logan thought my nipples were alert this morning, he's definitely going to notice them now.

Did this old woman really tell me I needed a shot?

I'm waiting for her to put the lid on and shake it, but instead she grabs the RumChata next and pours that in.

Now the lid goes on, and she aggressively shakes before pouring it into a rocks glass.

"It's supposed to be a shot, but it's your lucky day that I have a heavy hand," she tells me as she sets the glass down and walks away without another word.

Looking down at my drink, I can officially confirm that I was sent here for a shot.

I haven't drunk Fireball since college. And even then it was something I had to force down, knowing it would be coming right back up a few hours later.

"Well, I guess you only live once," I mumble to myself as I pick up the glass, throwing back the entire thing. If I didn't do it in one swoop, I wouldn't be going back for the rest.

The last thing I want is for the bartender to think I hate her drink. She wasn't rude, but she also wasn't overly friendly either. Her hard exterior reminded me of my mom in a way. Hardness always gets mistaken for just being plain worn out and tired.

"Whoa." My fist covers my mouth as I burp it down, my left eye squinting through the whole thing. "That's some Christmas cheer, all right."

It didn't taste as bad as I had been expecting. The RumChata masked some of the Fireball flavor and made it taste more like Cinnamon Toast Crunch. A very spicy Cinnamon Toast Crunch. I can feel the Fireball moving through the center of my body, warming it as it flows through and settling in my tummy.

"Atta girl," a man calls from his seat at the end as he holds up his draft beer in salute.

Great.

I'm new here and already causing a stir.

"Another round?" the bartender asks as she grabs my empty glass and places it in the sink.

"Oh, no thanks. I still have shopping to do. It was great, though." I smile a smile that I hope isn't wonky because I already feel the alcohol going to my head.

After settling my tab, I slide off the bar stool to head to my next destination. A flannel shirt for Logan.

I'm currently in the shop at the end of the street looking at a million different flannels. It's all the same style shirt, but who knew they came in every color combination imaginable?

If there's one thing I can take away from this trip, it's that northerners take their flannel very seriously.

"Need help finding anything, ma'am?" an older man asks as he approaches me.

I try my best to hide my cringe at him calling me ma'am.

"Do you have this one in an XL? I don't see any out here," I ask as I hold up the gray-blue and black flannel that reminds me of Logan's eyes.

I don't actually know if he's an XL, but there's no way a man his size would fit into anything smaller than a large. His biceps are basically the size of my thighs, for crying out loud.

The man does a show of looking through the sizes to double-check before taking off to see if there is more in the back.

I take the time to wander to see what else they have.

"Oh, Jesus fucking Christ." I laugh as I grab the hanger off the rack.

The old lady wasn't lying.

They really do have flannel underwear.

Putting it back on the rack, I flip through, looking at the different options and styles it comes in.

I've always been a thong girl through and through. I can't wear briefs without feeling like I have an adult diaper on.

Wait.

Is that…

Holy shit.

It's flannel lingerie.

The flannel set is red and black, much like the shirt Logan wears every day. The cups and thong are lined with a thin layer of black lace. The bra has a small amount of push-up in it so I know it will give the girls a lift.

"We have one left, ma'am. I can ring that up for you up front if you would like," the older man says as he comes back with the shirt for Logan.

"I'll take this too, please," I say as I hand him the lingerie before I register what just came out of my mouth.

I watch as the poor man's face turns beet red. I don't miss how he grabs the hanger with only two fingers from my hand and heads up front without another word.

God.

Way to go, Wynn.

Can you make this any more fucking awkward?

He rings me up in silence as I pray Logan is out there waiting for me so I can escape this area and never have to look this man in the eyes again.

I didn't think about getting Logan's number to see where he would be.

"Have a nice day," the old man mumbles as he hands me my bag.

"Thank you, you too." I clear my throat and make a beeline for the door.

The cold air nips at my face, but in this moment I welcome it. It's something to take the edge off what just happened.

My head turns to the right as I hear the sound of a truck door closing.

My lips tip into a smile as I watch Logan saunter over to me.

"You get all your shopping done, princess?" he asks when he reaches me, taking my bags from my hand.

Feeling like someone is staring at me, I turn around and notice the old man has his eyes locked on us.

Great.

Logan notices me staring and looks in the same direction and, to my horror, waves at the man.

Fucking waves.

"Did Gary take care of you?" Logan asks, turning his attention back to me.

"Gary?"

"Where you got this stuff from." He holds up the bag with his shirt and my lingerie.

"Oh. Yeah. He was really nice." I rush out as I try to take the bag out of his hand.

"I got it." Logan moves it out of my reach. "You ready to head back?"

"Yeah." I nod my head.

Please get me the fuck out of this street before I die of embarrassment.

CHAPTER
Eight

WYNN

It isn't until we're pulling into the driveway of the cabin that I realize I never had Logan take me to the grocery store.

I break the silence that had settled in the truck on the ride home by clearing my throat. "Um, I don't mean to sound needy or anything because you took me into town like I've been wanting—"

"Spit it out, princess." Logan cuts me off as he parks the truck in front of the garage.

"There's no food." I rush out. "There wasn't much in your fridge when I made dinner last night, and it completely slipped my mind to tell you we needed to stop at the grocery store. It's not completely my fault, though. I blame the Christmas cheer I was told to have without knowing what it was."

Logan moves in his seat, angling his body toward me as he cuts the engine. "Who told you to have some Christmas cheer?"

"I don't know. The lady who works in the shop that is stuffed full of the most random shit. She told me to stop there next. I thought it was more decor or something. I wasn't expecting a drink that made me feel like my nipples were going to slice through my bra."

Logan's eyes move to my chest, locking in.

The fur coat may be covering them now, but he's seen enough to envision what's hiding underneath.

"Norma talked you into it?"

"I didn't get a name, but she didn't talk me into anything because she didn't tell me what it was. Christmas cheer should come with a warning label."

"You look alright to me."

I roll my eyes. "Not the point, big guy."

Logan's lip tips up. "It's okay to let your hair down, Wynn. Norma telling you to go there is her way of letting you know she likes you. It's a locals thing. If she didn't like what she saw, she wouldn't have steered you in the right direction. And before you start freaking out about groceries, I stopped at the store before I came and picked you up. I know there wasn't shit in my fridge."

"You went grocery shopping?" I ask in disbelief.

I can't picture Logan doing a full shop. After all, I saw only beer, water, and meat in his fridge.

"Got all the essentials in the back. Let's get inside. It's getting cold."

Now that he says it, a shiver runs through me. The truck has chilled a lot since he cut off the heat.

Once we're inside, Logan heads to the kitchen area and sets the grocery bags down.

And by bags, I mean two.

Two bags doesn't say you went grocery shopping. Two bags is my three-hundred-dollar target run on shit I don't need.

"I thought you said you went grocery shopping?" I ask as I start to dig through the bags.

"I did," Logan says from the living room.

"Uh… all you've got is some sort of meat and potatoes," I say as I hold up the said meat wrapped in butcher paper in the air with my other hand on my hip.

"Yeah… What did you expect?"

I look at him in shock as I try to decide whether he's serious or not.

The look on his face is telling me that he is.

"I don't know, maybe some sort of vegetable or something to make an actual meal with." Or enough food for more than one meal.

I mean, come on. He can't seriously eat like this for every meal and still look like that.

"I'm a meat and potatoes man, princess. If I want to cook something else, I've got some cream soups in the cupboard. I can chop the steak up and make a casserole with it."

Cream soup and a casserole?

With chopped steak?

What in the world?

"I'm sorry, what?" I ask, unable to keep the shock mixed with a little disgust off my face.

"Cream of mushroom soup. It goes with everything."

Holy shit, I don't even know what to say.

"No, it absolutely does not go with everything. No one in their right mind should have that much cream unless you want to die at fifty or shit your brains out for the rest of your life."

"Don't tell my mom that." Logan laughs. "Her tuna noodle casserole has been feeding me since diapers."

Oh, Lord.

"I wouldn't insult your mom," I mumble as I put the groceries away, figuring I'm not winning this battle.

I always thought the idea of a mama's boy was cringe and a red flag, but honestly, it's cute the way he talks about her. You can tell she cares a lot about her family.

"You never said." Logan pauses to throw some logs into the fireplace. "Did you get anything good in town?"

My face heats at the memory that's still way too fresh.

"Yeah," I quickly reply. "There were some cute decorations in Norma's shop."

Among other things, I found along the way.

"You get more shit to decorate the cabin with?" Logan asks.

"No." Although by his tone now I wish I would have. "I brought all the stuff I need. The only thing left is baking."

"Like cookies?" Logan asks, perking up.

"Yes, like cookies." I roll my eyes. "Do you want a beer?" I ask as I grab the wine glass from the drying rack and empty the bottle from last night into it.

"If you're willing to grab me one, princess, I'll take it." Logan's reply comes just as the fire ignites, illuminating the room with the orange glow that's quickly becoming a comfort item to me.

Grabbing his beer out of the fridge, I make my way over to him and hold it out, waiting for him to take it. Once he does, I can't stop myself from slowly running my fingers through his hair, lightly scratching his scalp as I go.

Logan sets his beer down on the floor next to his knee as he leans back against it.

"That feels good," he rumbles.

"I always enjoyed having my head scratched. It's the one thing that will put me right to sleep." My fingers slowly drag from his forehead to the back of his head, lingering for a moment.

"I'd pay you every night to do this."

"You don't need to pay me."

I would do this every night if I could.

We're both lost in a trance from different sensations, his from the physical touch and mine from the act of service.

Logan is fully leaning back now. His back is resting against my shin, and his cheek is against my knee.

Just as I'm about to sit down next to him and have him lay down in my lap, the fire cracks and pops, shooting a spark out that flies right toward me, landing on the top of my hand that's scratching Logan's head, ruining the moment.

"Ouch!" I cry out, yanking my hand out of his hair.

"Shit, did it hit you?" Logan asks as he spins around and stands up in one fluid motion.

"Yeah," I whimper, tears already threatening to spill from the corner of my eyes as I cradle my hand to my chest, hoping the feeling like my skin is on fire will stop.

I hate that I'm such a baby with pain.

It's like my heart is made of ice with a stonewall around it so emotions don't hurt, but anything physical?

I'm a big fucking baby.

"Let me see it," Logan says, his voice lowering with concern as he reaches for my hand.

I jerk away from him on reaction, not wanting to remove my hand from my chest because in some fucked up space in my head it thinks me pressing it tight against my body is actually doing something to help.

"No," I say, sounding like the giant baby I am. "It's fine."

"It's clearly not fine if you're turning away from me. You wouldn't have tears in your eyes, princess," Logan says, his voice even.

He's trying to calm me down, but it's only semi-working.

"It's fine." I sniffle.

My whole hand feels like it's on fire now.

"Can we at least run it under some cold water?" he asks, trying to meet me halfway.

I sniffle and nod as I let him lead me over to the kitchen sink.

Logan turns the faucet on and holds his finger under the tap for a few seconds until he thinks it's cold enough. The coolness of his finger from the water makes me jump as it touches my wrist of the injured hand.

"You gotta let me have it so I can run it under water and get a look at it," Logan says, his voice laced with concern.

His gray-blue eyes are staring straight into my soul, making me forget for a second what had just happened. Concern etches his face as his brow lowers in concentration, making the lines in his forehead look even more pronounced as he brings his other slowly up to my face to wipe away the few tears that have slipped out of the corner of my eye.

I slowly release the tension in my arm, letting Logan move my hand under the water by the gentle hold he has on my wrist. The burn is already starting to blister, and the surrounding skin is beet red.

I whimper as the cold water hits my hand. It hurts and feels good at the same time.

Logan wraps his other arm around my waist, drawing me in closer to him until I'm pressed up against his side. Without warning, his lips touch my temple and linger there, giving me one of the slowest and most intimate kisses I've ever had in my life, and it wasn't even on my lips.

I should have backed away because we aren't there. I'm not even sure I know what there is. In my head, it's just a silly daydream. Kind of like the ones you have with the guy you're crushing on at the gym but will never have the guts to actually talk to.

I'm on sensory overload because he's everywhere. His scent is the only thing I can smell as he wraps me up tight in his one-arm hold. It's the smallest gesture, but somehow it feels like so much more than that.

We've shifted without realizing it, and I'm not sure if he's aware.

"Does it feel better?" Logan asks. "I shouldn't have had you so close to the fire with me."

"It's not your fault," I reply softly. "It only stings a tiny bit."

It actually stings a whole lot, but I'm not going to tell him that because he's already beating himself up over it when it was something out of his control.

"You're going to have a nice blister there for a while," Logan says, ignoring me telling him it's not his fault as he pulls my hand out from under the water and looks it over. "Good thing you've finished your decorating. I wouldn't want a gnome going rogue and popping open this blister."

And just like that, my tears have dried up and are no more as my body is shaking instead as I'm trying to contain my laugh. "A gnome would never do me dirty like that."

Logan grabs a hand towel off the counter and starts lightly tapping it onto my hand as he tries to dry my hand as gently as possible.

I can't stop staring at how his hand looks next to mine. It's almost double the size and is rough. There's just something that's incredibly fucking hot about a man who works with his hands like Logan does.

His fingers look like they have muscles, which is honestly insane.

He makes me feel so small and delicate, which I didn't think I would ever in a million years like, but I do.

I really fucking do.

Back home, I always go for the guy that's trying to climb the corporate ladder and would rather pay someone to do the manual labor than do it himself. Every single one of my exes acted like it was a flex and status symbol to say they had a lawn care company and a housekeeper.

Coming here has made me realize I've been looking for what I want out of life in all the wrong places.

"Did they tell you that?" Logan snickers as I roll my eyes. He throws the damp towel on the counter and examines my hand one last time, now that it's dry. "Now I really know you're feeling better if you can roll your eyes at me. When that sass I love so much is gone, that's when I know it's bad."

The sass he loves so much?

Trying my best not to be obvious about it, I quickly study Logan.

Am I wrong about him not realizing things have shifted?

Does he feel it too?

Oh, my God, I would die.

"Well, don't you worry. The sass is back in action and ready to put out gifts tomorrow."

"Gifts?" Logan's attention moves from my hand to my face.

I can feel my cheeks heating with embarrassment because how do I tell the guy I'm into that I went Christmas shopping for myself and wrapped everything I brought so I had something to open on Christmas morning.

"I brought some gifts to put under the tree. No one likes looking at an empty tree." There. That sounds good. And it's true. An empty tree just looks sad and pathetic.

"That's nice your family members sent what they got you with you."

A lump forms in my throat.

I told him briefly that I was doing this trip for my mom, but maybe he didn't pick up on the fact that it was always just my mom and me. Maybe he thought I usually travel to family for the holiday instead. People do that all the time, so I get the assumption.

Swallowing the lump in my throat, I worked up the courage to tell him the truth.

"Um, not exactly. I went shopping for myself and wrapped what I bought," I mumble, my left eye wincing as I spit it out.

The longer he studies my face with his soft expression, the more embarrassed I feel.

I don't want him to feel sorry for me.

I don't want or need pity looks.

That's exactly why I decided to take this trip and bail on crashing my friends' Christmas. I came here to escape the looks, and somehow, I landed smack dab in the middle of what I ran from.

"You don't have any family around?" Logan asks, his gentle

tone slowly eating me up inside.

"I told you it was just my mom and me," I answer softly.

"Well, yeah, but…" Logan trails off as I shake my head.

There has never been any other family for me. I never knew my dad and my mom had cut her side off before I was born. Every time I asked, she would get upset and change the subject, so eventually I stopped asking.

"I'm sorry, princess." Logan squeezes my side, pulling me in tight against him again.

My heart is supposed to be locked up with an impenetrable fortress built around it. No emotions are supposed to even come close to it.

So why am I feeling an immense sense of sadness that is making my chest feel tight?

"It's okay," I whisper, because what else is there to say?

"It's not, but we're going to make this a good one for you," Logan replies just as softly, placing another kiss on my temple.

This time his lips feel more wet and puckered. Like he did it with intention this time and not just in the heat of the moment because I injured myself.

"Let's go finish our drinks and enjoy the fire that almost took you away from me," Logan jokes, trying to lighten my mood.

A small smile spreads across my face, aimed right at his back as he heads into the living room.

I appreciate him more than he'll ever know.

I follow not far behind him into the living room and settle into my spot, the smile not leaving my face.

I'm starting to think I would follow this man just about anywhere.

CHAPTER Nine

WYNN

"How's your hand?"

That's the first thing Logan asks me when I walk down the stairs the next morning. Much to my shock, I woke up, and it was actually fully light out, meaning I didn't wake up at the ass crack of dawn to him chopping wood.

I was dead to the world last night. It could have been a combination of the wine and the pain pill Logan made me take because he saw me favoring my other hand, or the temple kiss he gave me right before I went up to bed.

Three temple kisses in one night had me feeling more relaxed than a bottle of Cabernet ever has.

"It feels better than it did last night," I answer as I join him in the kitchen.

"Let me see." Logan holds out his hand, waiting for me to place mine in his. He gently moves my hand from side to side, looking at the blister that's about the size of a nickel from every angle. "I think you'll survive."

"Gee, thanks." I roll my eyes.

Like I didn't know that.

The only thing I'm worried about now is popping that sucker open because blister puss grosses me the fuck out. Plus, they always burn really badly when that happens. I also don't want a nasty scar on my hand from a stupid burn.

"Coffee is on if you want any. Mugs are in the cupboard above the microwave," Logan says as he puckers his lips, blowing gently on the steaming black liquid.

"Thanks, but hot coffee isn't really my thing." I shudder at the thought.

Logan lowers the mug from my lips slightly as he looks back at me. "Please tell me you aren't one of those iced coffee all the time even if it's below freezing outside girls."

"Guilty." I smirk. "I mainly drink iced matcha, but occasionally I'll have an iced coffee if it isn't super sweet. I can drink them without cream, honestly."

"If you don't like the fru fru drinks, then why can't you have regular coffee?"

How do I tell him this without sounding like a complete psycho?

"It's not the coffee itself. It's the temperature. I don't like feeling hot liquid moving through my body. It makes me want to crawl out of my skin."

Logan stares at me for a moment as he tries to figure out how to respond.

"Good to know, princess. No hot morning coffees for you."

I give him a small smile as I lean up against the counter with my back to it.

"So what are you doing today if you aren't out playing lumberjack?"

"Playing lumberjack?" he repeats with his lip tipping up as he sets his coffee mug down on the counter.

"Yeah. Every single morning since I've arrived, all you've done is do something manly outside with your flannel on. Today is the first day you aren't doing just that."

"Doing something manly?" Logan is fighting laughter. "First off, I am a fucking man. And I do shit outside because if I'm inside for too long, I start to feel cooped up."

"I can't relate. I was born to live a life of leisure. Vegging on the couch and binging my comfort shows with all of my favorite snacks is good for the soul. You can't tell me otherwise."

"I wouldn't know. I've never tried it."

I'm not surprised in the slightest by that.

"Well, buckle up, big guy, because we're having a movie night on Christmas Eve. I already have it all planned out and everything."

"Great," Logan says, his tone laced with sarcasm that doesn't reach his eyes. Instead, his eyes are full of light and happiness. Almost as if he's excited about what I have planned.

"So what are you doing today?"

"Well, considering it's almost noon." Logan makes a show of looking at his watch. "Not much for the day, but tonight I'm meeting the boys."

Oh, yes. It's Friday.

"Is the man who you wanted to arrest me going to be there?"

Logan sighs. "I didn't want to have you arrested. But yes, Jackson will be there."

"What do you call that then?"

"I call it wanting to know who was in my fuckin' place at midnight. You scared the shit out of me."

"A big guy like you scared of little ole me?" I tease.

"Whatever," Logan grumbles, looking put out. "I was going to invite you tonight, but now I'm not."

My mouth drops open in a playful shock. "Rude. I would still have invited you if the roles were reversed."

Logan lets out a loud laugh. "No, the fuck you would not have. You would have probably stabbed me. I don't know if you remember what happened, but you were ready to go toe to toe with me. I didn't know whether to be pissed or turned on."

"Turned on. The answer is always turned on." I blurt out before I realize what I just said.

Shit.

"It is when it comes to you." Logan sets his empty mug in the sink. "Be ready by six."

I'm left speechless and unable to move from where my feet are planted on the kitchen floor.

I watched his fine ass strut out of the cabin after he just hit me with that blow.

He's so totally into me.

"Oh, shit," I say out loud.

What am I going to wear? I didn't bring my going-to-the-bar-with-a-lumberjack clothes because that was not on my bingo card for this trip.

I have to have something.

I'm the queen of overpacking. I probably brought enough outfits to last me a month, if I'm being honest.

Taking the stairs two at a time, I run to my suitcases that are open on the floor at the foot of the bed. I'm on a mission as I rip clothes out of my bag, discarding the items that just won't do over my shoulder.

By the time I'm done, it looks like a tornado went through the room, hitting only my suitcases.

At least I found an outfit.

Looking at the time on the old alarm clock that's on the nightstand, I see it's just after one p.m. That gives me five hours to get ready.

Definitely doable, and gives me time to wash my hair.

Am I going overboard in thinking this is a date?

Probably.

But even if it's not a date, I'm not one to go somewhere underdressed, even if it is a bar. I rather be overdressed for every occasion. You never know who you're going to run into.

Looking myself over in the mirror, I tuck a loose curl behind my ear.

I decided on a pair of dark denim jeans that hug every curve, a heather gray ribbed long-sleeve henley top I tucked into the jeans, all paired with a black belt that has a cute silver buckle to add extra flare. The Henley top is low-cut, showing off ample cleavage, and the jeans are doing things to my ass that even I have to take a second to appreciate.

I grab a small black clutch I packed just in case and throw my cards, ID and lip gloss into it before sliding on my black heeled boots, I zip up the sides and grab my fur coat, throwing it over my arm before heading for the stairs exactly five minutes before Logan told me to be ready.

"Are you not getting ready?" I ask Logan as I walk down the

stairs, noticing he's still in the same clothes as earlier.

"It's just a—" He looks up from his phone where he's sitting on the couch and pauses, his eyes flaring as they roam my body, making my breath catch in my throat. "Bar."

"Do I look okay?" I ask as I reach the bottom, Logan's eyes never leaving me. "You didn't tell me what type of bar this is, so I guessed on dress code."

Judging from Logan is still in the same outfit as this morning, I'm going to go out on a limb and guess I'm overdressed.

Logan clears his throat as he moves his attention from my chest to my face. "You look great, Wynn."

"Thanks," I reply softly, my cheeks warming at the compliment. It's nothing special, but coming from Logan, it means everything. "Are you ready to go?"

"Yeah. Let me grab my keys."

My eyes are glued to Logan's ass as I watch him walk away from me and toward the kitchen to nab his keys off the counter. He holds the front door open for me, letting me walk through first. I step through and wait for him to lock up.

He holds his arm out, and I take it as we walk down the porch steps and toward the truck, where he opens that door for me too.

I'm starting to think I wasn't overthinking this being a date because it sure feels like one.

I shiver as my butt touches the cold seat. Sometimes it feels impossible to get warm in this weather. I don't know if I could live in it.

"I should have started the truck twenty minutes ago. I'm sorry it's cold for you, princess."

My body might be cold, but my heart isn't.

"It's not your fault that it's cold as hell out here." I laugh lightly, trying to get a smile out of him as I place my hand on his bicep. It tightens under my touch, unintentionally making me squeeze slightly.

I've been dying to feel them since the moment I laid eyes on them. They're even better than I imagined.

"I'll have you warmed up soon." Logan's eyes are heated, making me think he means it in more ways than one.

Logan moves his arm to rest on the center console as he slowly starts to lean toward me. My brain turns to mush as I try to comprehend what's happening.

My gaze moves to his lips that I hope are heading my way.

Just as I start to tilt my head and meet him halfway, his phone starts ringing, ruining the moment.

Logan pulls back as he leans over on one hip to pull his phone out of his back pocket. "This isn't over," he rumbles.

I can practically feel the vibrations between my legs from the unsaid promise in the tone of his voice.

"Yeah?" Logan answers with his attention still on me.

"It's just after six, dude. Chill the fuck out. I'm on my way," Logan says into his phone.

Oops.

I guess I'm holding guys' night up.

"Yeah, I know it's my night to buy. Since when has that stopped you from starting a tab in my name?" Logan puts the truck in drive and pulls out onto the road to head toward town.

It just dawned on me that I'm in a vehicle old enough not to have Bluetooth. His phone doesn't even connect, so he can't talk through the car.

"Yeah, she's coming." Logan pauses as he listens to the guy on the other end. "Alright, bye."

"I'm not intruding on guys' night, am I? Because I don't have a problem staying home." In fact, I think I would prefer it. Going out with Logan sounds amazing, but going out with Logan and his friends? Now I'm nervous as fuck.

What if they don't like me?

"Hell no. Brody was just asking if you were coming because he brought his wife, Heather."

Hmmm. So, it's not just a guys' night then.

"Will any of the other wives be there?"

"Brody is the only one who is married. Jackson has a girl, but she went back to her hometown for the holidays because her sister is due any day."

"He didn't want to go with her?" I ask. I always thought it was weird when couples spend occasions apart like that.

"Couldn't. A con about being an officer in a small town is you're usually working holidays because there isn't someone to fill your spot."

"Damn, that sucks," I mutter as I look out the window.

The pictures online don't do this place justice. The snow covering the pine trees really does make it look like a winter wonderland. There's so much of it, it almost feels like I'm in a forest.

"It does, but he also knew what he was getting into when he took the job."

I can agree with that, as harsh as it may be.

"I'm sorry I made you late. I hope they aren't mad at me."

"You didn't make me late for shit, princess. And for the record, I would wait for you anywhere. If they're pissed about it, they can take it up with me." Logan's hand moves to rest on my upper thigh and gives it a light squeeze.

Looking down at his hand on me, I can't help but think it's the perfect hold. My hand moves to cover his, and that's how we stay the rest of the ride to the bar.

CHAPTER
Ten

WYNN

Logan pulls into a small parking lot and takes the last spot. The place is packed.

"Is everyone in town here?" I ask as he cuts the engine.

"Probably." Logan laughs, but something is telling me . he's actually serious. "There isn't much to do here in the winter unless you've got a sled or want to travel to ski or snowboard."

"If I run into Norma, I'm going to give her a piece of my mind for not being forthcoming with what Christmas cheer was," I say as I open my door and hop down.

"Go easy on the old woman. It's how she has her fun now."

Logan places his hand at the small of my back as we step up onto the sidewalk, nudging me along toward the front door with him following so close behind me that if it wasn't for my fur coat, I would be able to feel his body heat.

Logan reaches his arm around me, grabbing the door handle and opening it for me before applying a small amount of pressure to the small of my back as I walk through.

Stepping over to the side, I let him take the lead so my eyes can adjust to the dim lighting.

The decor is…wood.

That's the only way to describe it because it's covering the entire place.

The floors are wood; the tables are wood; the walls have wood paneling. Even the bar is made of wood.

And it's all the same yellowy brown color that's shiny from the topcoat covering it all.

The walls are covered with random mirrors with domestic beer logos on them and framed pictures of people. I'm assuming it's regulars or the owners.

Mounted deer heads are scattered around the walls, looking in every which way.

"They're in the back corner," Logan announces as he starts weaving in and out of the tables, leaving me to follow him blindly.

I don't miss the stares from the patrons as we pass. I'd like to think it's because Logan is so hot it's almost impossible to not stare at him, single or not, but I know that's not it.

I'm the only one not in a Carhartt coat.

The black fur makes me stick out like a sore thumb.

"I see you two decided to work it out," Jackson greets us as we approach their table.

"He hasn't tried to have me arrested again, so I guess you can say we've worked it out." I laugh as I slide into the chair Logan pulled out for me.

"I didn't try to have you arrested," Logan grumbles as he sits next to me.

I'm never going to let him live this down.

I look at him, unable to keep the smile off my face. "If that's what you want to go with."

"What can I get the two of you to drink?" the waitress asks. "I'm assuming you want your usual, Warner?"

"Please," Logan answers as he lays his arm behind my back so it's resting on the top of the back of my chair, directing his question at me. "What do you drink at bars? I know it's not red wine."

I roll my eyes at him before smiling at the waitress, who is staring at me expectantly. "Gin and soda with a lime, please."

She writes my order down on her little notepad before taking off.

Logan's brows shoot up.

"What?" I ask.

"Nothing. I just wasn't expecting you to say that."

"Yuck." Jackson's nose scrunches in disgust. "Who drinks gin? It tastes like a goddamn pine tree."

"Considering you're drinking a Natural Light, I don't think you have any room to comment on what I'm drinking," I sass, giving it right back to him.

The table erupts in laughter.

"I think you're going to fit in just fine, princess," Logan whispers in my ear. His warm breath tickles the inside of my ear, sending a shiver down my spine.

Logan slides my chair closer to his as he leans back up.

"Since Logan is so goddamn rude, I'm Brody." A man who looks like Logan, just a little bit heavier set and with blond hair, smiles at me. "And this is my wife, Heather." He points his thumb at the gorgeous redhead sitting next to him.

"Hi." I smile and shout over the noise. "It's nice to meet you."

"Oh, girl, I've been dying to meet you. Once Brody told me that Logan had shacked up with a girl, I just had to see you for myself. He did good." Heather winks at me.

Shacked up?

I turn to Logan looking for I don't know what… maybe some sort of backup in this situation considering he knows them and I don't, but Logan is looking the other way, almost as if he's ignoring me on purpose.

Not one to cause a scene in public. I let him pretend like he didn't hear what was just said… for now.

"Oh, we aren't shacked up." I wave it off. "I'm originally from Virginia and here for the holiday."

"Oh." Heather's smile wavers slightly. "Well, so many people do long distance now. It's the new thing."

New thing?

What the fuck is this woman talking about?

Is she really trying to tell me that long-distance relationships are trending right now after I just told her that's not what this is?

Maybe there's something in the water here.

"Drinks are up," the waitress announces as she sets them down in front of Logan and me. "Holler if you guys need another round."

"We've known Logan for years and never see him with anyone," Heather continues on. "We're just excited to see he found someone."

I cast a sideways glance at Logan, who is still suspiciously quiet as he takes a drink of his beer.

"We're just friends," I say, trying to get through to her. Honestly, I don't even know if I would call us friends yet.

Heather's brows raise as she tries to put the tiny black cocktail straw in her mouth but misses. "Really? Could have fooled me. You both walked in looking pretty cozy."

Deciding it's best to act like I didn't hear her before I start to get annoyed, I get the tiny black cocktail straw in my mouth on the first try and take a few gulps instead of responding.

I can't talk back if my mouth is full.

There isn't a lull in the conversation around us. The guys pick right up talking about random things happening around town and the amount of snow that's expected to come this weekend. I can't imagine getting more snow than there is now. It already hits my mid-calf.

Before I know it, I've sucked down my entire drink during my effort of not talking to Heather about Logan and me, and he's flagging down the waitress for another round.

It isn't that I don't want to talk to her; it's just that Logan and I are none of her business.

I mean, I don't even know what we are or if there even is a we.

It feels like it at times, but I've always been a realistic person. And reality is going to hit in about a week and a half when I have to go back home and Logan stays here. It feels like I have a devil on one shoulder telling me to go for it because what do I have to lose while on the other shoulder there's an angel telling me not to cross a line I have zero business crossing.

But dammit, I'm so sick of always doing what's predictable. Or what people think I should do.

I broke the cycle coming here, so it only seems fitting to continue it.

"You havin' fun?" Logan asks, interrupting my thoughts, his lips inches from my ear.

"Yeah. Your friends are easy to talk to." I half lie. The guys are easy, but that's how it's always been with me.

I've never been a girl's girl for the sole fact that I've never been able to maintain friendships with multiple women. I'll never be that girl who has a posse to call when shit hits the fan. The conversation with Heather is the perfect example of why I can barely do it. I don't like people prying into my personal life when they have no business doing it.

I have one close friend back home and, by extension, I've been inducted into her and her husband's friend group, but even that is surface level.

"I know Heather can be a lot sometimes, but she means well," Logan continues to say in my ear, sensing my slight distress with the situation.

I'm sure she does.

Maybe this next drink will loosen me up.

"Are we getting a round of shots or what?" Jackson asks the waitress loudly as she sets our next round down in front of us and nabs the empties.

"And how do you ask, officer? I know your mama didn't raise you in a barn," she fires back.

"Please," he adds with his eyes glimmering, his cheeks a light shade of pink from the alcohol.

"All of you?" she asks as she looks around the table.

I don't have a chance to shake my head before Logan quickly nods his, and she's off to make the rest of her rounds.

Now it's my turn to lean over into Logan, whispering in his ear so I don't sound like a pathetic bitch bowing out. "I don't think I can handle a shot."

Logan's head tilts toward me with his gaze cast downward. "You handled one yesterday just fine."

I try to contain the goosebumps that pepper my skin from his breath tickling my face, but I fail miserably.

"That was all I had, though. I'm a lightweight. If I start mixing, you're going to be carrying me up to bed," I say, still whispering as I look into his eyes.

Logan stares at me for a beat before he rocks my world. "If I carry you upstairs, I'm staying in that bed with you."

I cross my leg over the other as heat rushes between my thighs from his whisper, dropping an octave. He doesn't miss the change in my body language, but then again, there isn't much Logan doesn't miss.

"You'd like that, wouldn't you." It's not a question. "In case you were wondering if I'd like it too, you sleeping just a few feet away from me in my bed has been doing my head in. You let out these little moans and whimpers in your sleep that I can hear from the couch. You want to know why I've been up chopping wood at the ass crack of dawn every morning? It's because I need something to take the edge off since I can't be buried deep inside you."

Holy.

Fucking.

Shit.

My face is flushed, and it's not from the alcohol.

It's from this lumberjack of a man bulldozing his way into my Christmas vacation and tilting my world upside down.

"Shots!" the waitress yells over the loud music as she slams the glasses down in front of each of us, breaking us out of the moment. "Drink up!"

Logan only leans away slightly this time as he slides my shot glass toward me and picks up his, holding it in the air to cheers. "To great friends and women who walk around in fur coats."

I have no choice but to clink my glass against everyone's as I go through the motions. I'm the last to slam mine back and once I do, I'm immediately sent into a coughing fit.

"Whew." Heather fans her face as she looks between Logan and me with a knowing look. "I don't know if it's the alcohol doing its thing, but I could cut the sexual tension between the two of you with a knife."

Shit.

Were we that noticeable?

I know I felt it. Hell, I can still feel it.

"Keep doing what you're doing because that means I'm getting something sweet tonight." Brody winks before wrapping his arm around Heather and pulling her in close to him.

"Lucky bastards," Jackson grumbles as he slams his shot glass down.

Logan winks and doesn't push the subject anymore.

The rest of the night passed without any more conversations that made me squirm in my seat. The sexual tension never left. If anything, I think it intensified because after the third round of drinks, which Logan bowed out of with the excuse he had to drive so he can't even blame it on the alcohol, somehow his hand found its way to my upper thigh.

I then had to endure another hour and a half of torture. And by torture, I mean having to feel his hand rub up and down my thigh, squeeze my thigh and do just about anything with my thigh to drive me insane.

I swear his thumb brushed over the spot between my legs that's aching for him ever so lightly. So lightly that I almost thought my mind was playing tricks on me, but the little smirk on his face while he was talking to the guys gave it away.

I hope he knows payback is a bitch.

And it's going to hit him so hard he isn't going to know it's coming.

Through all of this, I tried my best to keep up the conversation with Heather, but it was so goddamn hard. I found myself saying yeah and nodding along when I had no clue what she was even talking about. If she could tell Logan was slowly torturing me under the table, she didn't let on.

Thank God.

I would have died of embarrassment on the spot.

I've never been a huge PDA girl. It's always given me the ick when I see someone basically fucking when I'm trying to eat while I'm out.

The pressure from his hand on my thigh increases as he leans over to whisper in my ear, "You about ready to head out of here?"

My senses are on overdrive.

Logan is everywhere.

I feel like I'm about to combust if I don't get this layer of clothing that's separating him from touching me and me touching him off of both of us.

I pick up my glass and slam the last half back before tilting my head. Our lips are centimeters from touching as I whisper back, "Take me home, big guy."

CHAPTER
Eleven

WYNN

f Heather had thought there was sexual tension at the bar, she probably would have had an orgasm on the spot if she were in the truck with us.

This time, it's my hand on Logan's thigh as he drives us back to the cabin. I'm rubbing him the same way he was rubbing me, except more.

A thrill runs through my body every time I feel his muscles clench and tighten under my touch. I don't have to travel that far until I feel what I've been searching for.

He's long, thick, and so fucking hard.

He feels exactly how I imagined him to.

And I can't wait to unwrap him.

The alcohol is giving me the courage I need to tell the angel on my shoulder to fuck off as my thumb circles around the head of his cock that's resting against his leg.

Logan sharply inhales as his hand leaves the steering wheel, gripping my wrist and halting my descent.

"Don't start something you aren't prepared to finish, princess," Logan's voice, low with need, rumbles throughout the truck, making every part of my body alert.

"Who says I'm not prepared?" I reply, the same need echoing in my tone as I give his weeping head another swirl on my thumb.

Logan's head falls back against the headrest, the tendons in his neck bulging as he roughly inhales through his nose as his hand on the steering wheel tightens.

I must have come out victorious with whatever internal battle he was having with himself because suddenly he releases the grip he had on my wrist without another word, giving me the green light.

Inside, I'm scared as shit while also feeling like a bad bitch for winning over this man. He's nothing like the men I've met before, and that scares the shit out of me. I'm so out of my comfort zone, it isn't even funny.

I wrap my hand around as much of his cock as I can through his jeans and run my hand up and down, applying pressure as I go.

"Fuck," he groans. "I hope you're ready for payback."

"Pot meet kettle." It's only fair.

Jesus, he's been hiding a monster in there.

"What?" Logan grunts out. He wound his body tight.

"You were teasing me all night under the table!" I accuse. He knows exactly what he was doing. The fucking tease.

"That was foreplay, princess. Your hands on me is a new form of hell because all it makes me want to do is pull this truck over, throw you in the backseat and eat you like I'm fucking starved." My breathing is coming in short pants. I want that. Holy shit, do I want that. "But I'm not going to do that because once I'm in there, that pussy is mine. And in this town, people stop to check on each other if they see you pulled over on the side of the road. If someone sees what's mine, well, I'd probably have to kill them."

My chest grows tighter as I cling to every word that leaves his lips.

"Yours?" I gulp.

I've never been someone's before. I've seen it happen to friends, but I never thought it would happen to me.

But Logan saying it?

I want it.

"Mine."

Logan turns sharply into the driveway of the cabin, sending me practically flying into his lap. The bed of the truck drifts before Logan spins the wheel quickly and rights it. He slams on the brakes, and we slide to a stop right in front of the garage. Logan throws the truck into park and cuts the engine as I push up off of him, slapping my palms on the center console and look at him with wide eyes because what the fuck was that?

"Don't move," Logan orders, ignoring me as he throws open his door and struts around the front of the truck until he reaches my door.

Throwing that open, too, he reaches around me and unbuckles my seatbelt before I have time to wrap my head around what's happening. The seatbelt slaps against the paneling; the sound echoing throughout the night.

Logan bends as one arm slides under my knees and the other behind my back before he's throwing me over his shoulder.

"Logan!" I screech. "What are you doing?"

Ignoring me, he kicks my door shut and struts up to the cabin. Once inside, he kicks his boots off without dropping me somehow before he's walking up the stairs to the loft with me still over his shoulder.

Holy shit, this is really happening.

Logan throws me down on the bed hard enough that I bounce back slightly. Pushing up on my elbows, I stare at him in shock.

He still hasn't said one word to me, but he's here.

Jesus Christ is he here.

The heat in his gaze is burning a hole into my body in a way that I will never recover from as he unbuttons one wrist of his flannel before moving on to the next. The moonlight coming in from the windows is illuminating the room, making his enormous frame somehow seem even bigger as he stands at the end of the bed, practically towering over me. He looks like he wants to devour me.

"Take your coat off, princess." Logan finally breaks the silence, his rumble vibrating throughout the room.

Or maybe just me.

I've never whipped my coat off so fast before as I flung it to God knows where. All I care about in this moment is watching Logan unbutton his shirt button by button, revealing the body I've missed since the night I got here at a painstaking, leisurely pace.

The ink I got a brief glance of is slowly coming into view, making my mouth water. Shifting my weight to one arm, I raise the other and use my finger to tell him to come here.

"Nu uh." Logan shakes his head, making my eyes narrow. He

can't be serious right now. "After that little stunt you pulled in the truck, princess, you haven't earned anything yet."

Oh, he really can't be serious right now.

"After the little stunt you pulled at the bar, you're lucky I'm telling you to come and get it," I fire back.

Logan's flannel is fully unbuttoned, and he's now pulling it off with his arms behind his back in the way all the hot guys do it in the movies as a low smirk spreads across his face.

"Me?" Logan tries to feign innocence as he undoes his belt.

"You know exactly what you were doing."

"I know what you're not doing," Logan replies, and his belt hits the floor.

"What's that?"

"Taking your fucking clothes off. Or do I need to do that for you?" His voice drops to the octave I love, the same one he used in the bar.

Even when this vacation fling fizzles out, it will remain permanently etched in my memory. I don't know how or when he did it, but he's wormed his way in in the most permanent way possible.

"I think you need to come over here and do it for me." My eyelids lower as I watch his hands go to the button on his jeans. "I think it would make up for what you did."

"Yeah? And what is that I did?" The zipper of his jeans sliding down echoes throughout the loft, sounding almost erotic.

"Tease me. Like what you're doing right now."

Logan's jeans hit the floor, leaving him in nothing but a pair of black boxer briefs that outline everything I was feeling in the truck.

And I mean everything.

Stepping out of the jeans, he puts a knee on the end of the mattress as he starts to crawl over me. "I guess I better make it up to you, eh?"

"That'd be the nice thing to do," I whisper.

I'm so far in over my head with this man it's not even funny, but that's not going to stop me from getting what I want.

And what I want is that mammoth python he's been packing in those tight-ass jeans.

Once he's inches from my mouth, Logan places his large,

rough hand on my chest, leaving me with no choice but to fall back on the bed with him looming over me.

Just as I'm about to ask if he's going to follow through or continue to be the big fat tease he's proven himself to be, with his breath on my lips, that same rough hand that pushed me down slides under my shirt and grasps my hip.

My body reacts by arching into him, the area where I need him the most making contact with his hard cock.

A long groan leaves Logan's lips as he grinds his hips into mine, pushing me back down into the mattress. His hand leaves my hip, trailing across my belly. His calloused fingers send a shiver down my spine and goosebumps cover my skin.

"My princess is so responsive," Logan rumbles as his hand continues its mission upward toward my breasts. "Let's find out if my touch can make her fly."

Inside, I'm screaming that he can. He's the only one who can. But my thoughts are a jumbled mess, and all I can think about is Logan.

Logan, Logan, Logan.

The same calloused fingers lightly trail between my breasts, making me push them up toward him, desperate for his touch.

In one quick swoop, he dives into my bra, swirling around my nipple before giving it a hard tug.

My mouth parts open on a moan at the same time his mouth slams down on mine, swallowing any noise I make. My hands are in his hair, tugging and pulling like I can't get enough as his tongue dominates my mouth.

It isn't much of a fight. He already owns every inch of me.

Logan grinds down again, his hard cock pressing in. My hands leave his hair and work their way in between us, trying to find the button on my jeans because I need them off.

The fact that he's basically naked except for his boxers and I'm still fully clothed is a new form of torture I didn't know existed. I don't think I've ever needed to have skin to skin contact so badly in my life.

Logan pulls back ever so slightly, breaking the kiss and leaving me breathless as he pushes his pelvis into me, holding me down against the mattress as his hand leaves my breast and grabs onto my wrist, holding that in place too.

"What do you think you're doing?" Logan rumbles.

"Taking my clothes off," I almost whine.

"You think you deserve that?"

"I need to feel you," I reply, looking at him with wide, pleading eyes, fully aware of how desperate I sound. "And you told me to."

I'm past the point of caring.

I'll beg if I have to.

"I'll never deny my princess what she needs," Logan says, his tone gravely.

Pushing up so he's on his knees in the bed, he holds his hands out for me to grab. I don't keep him waiting as I put my hands on his. They swallow mine as he folds his around mine and tugs, pulling me up into a sitting position.

He wastes no time grabbing the hem of my shirt and whipping it over my head, leaving me in a black lace bra. His eyes zero in on my nipples; he can see through the material since there's no padding.

"Jesus Christ," he growls. "You had that on all night sitting beside me?"

"Why don't you take these jeans off and find out what else I've had on all night while sitting next to you, big guy," I answer as I draw my bottom lip between my teeth.

His attention darts from my breasts to my mouth, watching every movement.

"And you think I'm the fucking tease," he mumbles to himself.

Logan makes quick work of undoing my jeans and pulling them down my legs. I help him out by kicking, by shuffling my feet against each other until the jeans are off. Logan's hand trails down my leg, squeezing my calf muscle as he goes. His hand feels rough against my soft foot as he grabs it and brings it to his mouth, softly kissing the top of it.

His hungry gaze roams back up my body but stops when he sees the tiny black triangle G-string that matches the bra.

My belly flutters as his nostrils flare.

His finger dives under the tiny scrap of material, sliding up my slit, making my head fall back and my mouth part open as a silent moan slips out.

"Fucking drenched." I watch through heavy-lidded eyes as Logan takes his finger and puts it into his mouth, sucking my arousal off.

Without warning, Logan yanks hard on the panties, snapping the tiny strings around my waist in half before he dives, heading straight to my pussy.

"Holy shit." I gasp, pushing my hips into his face as my hand goes straight to his head, fingers threading through his hair.

He's feasting as if he hasn't dined in years. It's been so long for me that I can already feel that familiar tingle I've been craving from him since the moment I laid eyes on him.

Jesus Christ this man knows how to use his fucking tongue.

My moans are getting louder the closer I get to toppling over the edge. I cry out as his tongue applies the right amount of pressure to my clit. I'm right there. I just need…

"No," I cry out as Logan pulls away. I try to push his head back down, but he resists. "Don't stop."

"You're not coming without me, princess." Logan reaches over me and into the nightstand, pulling out a strip of condoms.

If he didn't look so hot ripping one off with his teeth, I'd find the time to be pissed he has that many ready to go.

I lick my lips as I watch Logan give his hard cock a long stroke before rolling the condom on.

Running a finger through my slit again, I chase his finger with my hips.

"Hurry," I plead. "Don't make me wait anymore."

"Shhh," Logan whispers. "I'm not making you wait, but I need to make sure you're ready to take me."

Just as I'm about to protest, two thick fingers circle my entrance before dipping in. It's frenzied from there. He's pumping them in and out at a fast pace, scissoring them every which way as he stretches me.

The familiar high I was chasing moments earlier is back with a vengeance. Logan hears it from my cries and abruptly pulls his fingers out and replaces them with the head of his cock.

"Eyes on me, Wynn," Logan rumbles as he looks down at me. The veins in his neck and arms are strained from the control he's barely holding on to.

Looking up into his heated blue-gray eyes, my mouth parts open as my breath catches in my throat at the feel of him pushing inside. He makes it a few inches before pulling out and pushing back in. It's a tight fit that brings the slightest pinch.

A few more thrusts and my walls flutter around him at the feeling of his throbbing cock.

It's perfect.

"Jesus fucking Christ," Logan groans, his forehead collapsing against mine, eyes closed.

Only our mingled breathing is heard throughout the cabin.

"Logan?"

"Yeah," he gets out through clenched teeth.

"Move."

He picks his head up off mine as he leans back to look into my face. The tight pinch I felt when he first entered me is gone. I feel full. Full of Logan. He's in the last place that was untouched by him. He touched it in a way that I know I will never be the same after this.

Logan pulls all the way out and slams back in, doing this motion over and over, setting a frenzied pace. I drag my nails down his scalp and neck until I reach his back, digging in harder, leaving my mark on him as I continue the descent to his ass.

Logan shoves his face in my neck, biting down on my collarbone the deeper my nails dig into his skin.

My moans are getting higher, and his breathing is getting heavier. He hears the hitch in my voice and, sliding a hand between us, his thumb going to my clit, pressing in just right, sending me over the edge.

A long groan leaves Logan's lips as my walls flutter around him, clenching him in tight and sending him over the edge.

Logan lazily thrusts in and out as we both come down. He places light kisses along my neck and collarbone as he caresses my side. Once our breathing has evened out, he slips out of me, falling on his side next to me before he's pulling me in his arms, wrapping me up tight.

"You good?" he asks softly, placing a soft kiss on my temple.

"Yeah," I reply just as softly. "I've been wanting to be wrapped up in you since the night you tried to have me arrested."

His chest shakes beneath me. "You're never going to let that go, are you?" His voice sounds sated.

"No."

How could I?

It's either going to go down as the best meet-cute in history, or it's going to be the waving red flag I should have listened to and turned my ass right back around and found somewhere else to stay.

"You're lucky I just came the hardest I have in my fucking life. I'm too mellow to get worked up by your sass." His hand lightly taps my ass.

"The hardest you've ever come?" I ask, trying to keep the gloating out of my tone.

It was really good.

Like really fucking good.

"I don't know if you've caught on or not, princess, but our sexual chemistry lights up a room. Even Heather wouldn't shut up about it. I knew it was going to be good when I finally got in there. I just didn't know it was going to be so good that you marked me in a way that I know I'll never have better than you."

My chest tightens at his admission.

It's one thing to have those feelings about another person, but it's a whole different feeling to hear they feel the same way, especially when they admit it first.

Logan sighs, mistaking my silence as a bad sign. "I know we aren't there yet, and we haven't talked about what this is, but I'm a straightforward guy. If I feel it, I lay it out there. I'm not expecting you to declare your undying love for me, but just know that you're in there."

"It's not that… it's… I feel the same," I finally get out.

And that's fucking crazy because in reality I barely know the guy. I'd be a fucking idiot to deny the connection we have though.

His chest, which I didn't realize had tightened beneath me, instantly relaxes on my admission.

"Good." Logan pulls the covers over us, tucking them in around me before placing one last kiss on my temple. "Sleep, princess."

On command, I find myself closing my eyes and having the best sleep of my life.

CHAPTER
Twelve

WYNN

The next morning, I woke up to an empty bed. His pillow is still warm, so I know he hasn't been gone long.

Rolling onto my back, I stretch my arms above my head, causing the covers to slide down until they're barely covering my nipples as I hear the toilet in the adjoining bathroom flush and the bathroom door open, revealing a tattooed Logan in nothing but boxer briefs.

Yummy.

"My eyes are up here." Logan smirks as he saunters back to bed.

"I didn't get to admire you last night in the dark," I say, turning on my side and propping my head up in my hand with an elbow to the bed.

"Admire away. I won't complain." Logan tucks his hands behind his head as he leans against the headboard.

All of his tattoos are black and gray. I wouldn't say he has a lot; they're just bigger, so it looks like a lot. He has a family crest with Warner covering one of his pecs. One of his arms is covered with random skulls fading into pine trees.

With a mind of its own, my free hand reaches out, tracing the family crest on his chest.

"When I woke up and saw you weren't next to me, I thought you might be out chopping wood," I tell his chest, not meeting his eyes.

"I told you I was only doing that to work out not being in you. Now that I've got you, I'm only chopping wood when I need it."

"That's too bad." I hum. "I kind of enjoyed watching you do it in your flannel."

"If that's what gets you going, princess, we can go outside and I'll start chopping right now."

"Yeah." I smile, raising my gaze to his face. "I have stuff to do this morning, but I'll take a raincheck."

Logan's brow lowers as he starts lightly stroking the hand I have on his chest. "What could you possibly have to do today? You're on vacation and I'm the only one you know here."

"Not true. I know Heather, Brody, and Jackson."

"They don't count."

I let out a laugh. "I think Heather would disagree. But if you must know, big guy, I have presents to wrap and put under the tree. I also want to go into town and get some stuff to make cookies."

"I'll take you."

"You don't need to do that. The roads seem pretty clear now."

"It snowed last night. I don't trust your tiny fucking car to make it. You're lucky you made it here and didn't end up in a ditch somewhere."

"I made it here just fine," I say as I plop on my back with an eye roll.

I made it here. Barely. But he doesn't need to know how many times I almost went off the road and screamed because I thought I was going to die.

"Uh huh," Logan mutters. The smile in his voice has me narrowing my eyes. "Let's get around and I'll take you into town."

I'm about to protest but think better of it because if he's not lying about it snowing overnight, I don't want to drive in it. Snow in Michigan is nowhere near what the snow in Virginia is like.

"Okay," I reluctantly agree as I throw the covers off of me.

A shiver runs through my body from the cold air hitting my skin. One thing I'll never get used to is how cold it is inside in the morning before Logan lights a fire. It's almost criminal that people can live like this.

"I'll get a small fire going," Logan says to my back, having watched me shiver. "Why don't you go shower and warm up?"

Sliding off the bed, I can feel Logan's eyes on me as I make my way over to the bathroom, not bothering to cover up. Pausing in the doorway, I lean up against the doorframe. Turning my head, I look over my shoulder at Logan, throwing him a sultry smile. "Don't you want to get warmed up, too?"

Logan stares at me for a beat before he's whipping the covers off of him and rushes off the bed toward me.

I dash into the bathroom, giggling as I reach the shower, turning the handle clockwise. I shriek as Logan's cool hands grab my waist and spin me around as he backs me up against the wall.

"You going to warm me up?" Logan asks as he closes in on me.

"I'm going to do my best," I reply, my arms wrapping around his neck.

Logan's eyes flare before he crashes his lips to mine. I moan into his mouth as I open for him. He doesn't waste any time slipping his tongue inside, dominating the kiss. Possessiveness oozes out of him with every flick of his tongue.

Steam from the water is swirling around us, warming the bathroom.

Logan is the one to break the kiss, pulling away with a hungry look on his face.

"Let's get you warmed up," Logan's rumble echoes throughout the bathroom as he pulls the shower curtain back, releasing a big puff of steam. "After you." He waves his hand toward the water.

My eyes roam his body, locking on his tight ass as I brush past him and step into the shower.

Logan follows me, crowding me up against the shower wall as he closes the curtain. It's a tight fit for both of us in here. His large frame barely fits in here, the water spraying from the shower head only hitting the top of his shoulder blades.

"Come here," he murmurs. His hands land on my hips as he holds me in place against the wall.

He leans in, making me think he's going to kiss me breathless again, but instead he goes for my neck, placing wet kisses down and along my collarbone.

I tilt my head to the side to give him better access as my hands make their way to his ass, giving it a tight squeeze that earns me a groan. He thrusts his hips toward me, making me gasp as his hard cock nestles its way between my legs with nowhere else to go.

Logan drops to his knees, making me lose the grip I have on

his ass.

"What are you doing?" I ask, sounding breathless.

"I need to taste you."

My hands slam against the shower wall, the slapping noise echoing throughout the bathroom as Logan's tongue assaults my pussy. That's the only way to describe it. He's dining like he hasn't eaten in days when in reality he had me not even twelve hours ago.

Logan's tongue swirls around my clit as he alternates between suckling and flicking. My head slams back against the wall. Pain radiates through my head, but I don't register it.

All I can feel is Logan.

I tug on his hair, egging him on as he growls into my pussy, the vibrations igniting the tingling sensation only he can give me.

I'm close.

I pull harder on Logan's hair, silently letting him know that I need more.

"You ready for me, princess?" Logan asks as he breaks away from my pussy and looks up at me while he's still on his knees. His beard is glistening, and it's not from the water pelting us.

"You know I am." Logan smirks as I look down at him through heavy-lidded eyes.

Standing to his feet, he reaches above me and grabs a condom off the little corner ledge of the shower.

I eye him, wondering when in the hell he put that there.

"What?" Logan shrugs as he rips it open with his teeth. "I knew if I followed your sexy ass in here, I would need something."

"Aren't you sure of yourself."

Logan rolls the condom onto his dick before grabbing my leg and wrapping it around his waist. "Always when it comes to you."

Logan slams in without warning. My walls flutter around him as my head falls onto his shoulder. He hikes my other leg up, telling me to wrap him up without words.

And wrap him up, I do.

I'm holding on for dear life as his hands go under my ass to hold me up against the wall. It isn't the best position as he can't pull all the way out, but the angle is a whole new level. With every shallow thrust, he brushes against my clit.

"Oh my God," I cry out as he hits the same spot over and over again.

"You going to come with just my cock?" Logan asks in between grunts as my walls clamp down around him in a vice grip. "Fuck yeah."

I explode around Logan with a cry, taking him over the edge with me. His mouth slams down on mine as I swallow his grunts.

Logan lazily thrusts in and out as his cock softens and my body relaxes around him. With one arm under my ass, he uses the other to unlock one of my legs from around him and lowers it to the ground.

His palm rubs the side of my thigh that's still wrapped around him. "You warmed up yet?"

A laugh bubbles out of me as I look up at Logan. "Yeah, you warmed me up. Thank you." I kiss him, sucking his bottom lip into my mouth before letting it go with a pop.

Logan grabs my body wash off the ledge and pops open the cap, pouring some into his hand.

"What are you doing?" I ask, watching him lather the soap between his hands.

"Washing you." He spreads the lathered soap across my chest and down my arms first, slowly working his way down my body, massaging me as he goes. "Feel good?"

"Yes…" I trail off on a soft moan.

It's been so long since I've had any sort of physical contact that my body feels like Jell-O. The tightness that I was beginning to think was never going to leave my body has somehow melted away.

Who would have thought the cure was a six-foot five lumberjack in Northern Michigan?

Logan steps to the side so the spray is fully hitting me. I watch the soap bubbles slide off my body and down the drain as he washes his own body. He presses up behind me so we're both in the spray as he rinses himself off. Reaching over my shoulder, he turns the faucet off.

"Stay put. I'll grab some towels." Logan darts out, making a mad dash to grab us towels.

Even though the shower was hot, the bathroom air still feels ice cold as it hits my skin. Wrapping my arms around myself, I try to contain my shiver.

"Here." Logan returns with a towel wrapped around his waist as he holds one open for me to step in to. Once I do, he wraps it around me, and suddenly I don't feel so cold anymore.

"Get ready and we'll head into town. I'll make a fire when we get back," Logan says as he exits the bathroom to leave me to it.

I know this is a vacation fling, but life with him just feels so easy.

Something tells me we've changed in a way that I'm not sure either of us is ready for.

CHAPTER
Thirteen

WYNN

Logan stayed true to his word and took me to the store for baking supplies to make cookies.

I may have gone overboard. After all, it is only the two of us.

Do two people need four kinds of cookies when each batch makes a couple dozen?

No.

But am I going to eat myself into a cookie coma, anyway?

Yes.

This will be the true test of judgment. He's either with the junk food binge or he's against me.

He followed me around the entire store and didn't complain once or ask why I was getting so many bags of Rolos when I'm only using them to make 24 cookies. He doesn't need to know that I end up eating a bag myself while unwrapping them during the prep stage. Logan is about to witness the glory of Christmas baking firsthand.

My mom used to get so mad at me whenever we made these because I would eat all the candy and then there wasn't enough to make cookies with, so they ended up being basic sugar cookies.

Logan also shoved my hand out of the way when I went to pay for everything. When I protested, his reasoning was: "Look at the size of me compared to you. Who do you think is going to be eating most of these, princess?"

That stopped any protest and snapped my mouth shut because the thought of Logan binging Christmas cookies with me and watching shitty movies on the couch sounded like it was going to be the best night I've had in a long time, not counting last night of course.

I don't think anything will ever top that night.

There's something more intimate in spending time with someone doing something that's personal to you versus spending time doing something that everyone does, like going out to dinner.

The second time I tried to protest was when Logan wouldn't let me bring any bags in once we arrived back home. He looked downright insulted when I opened up the back door and reached for the bag, telling me to get my fur coat covered ass in the cabin.

Who was I to argue with that?

Which leads us to now, me leaning up against the counter as I watch Logan carry all the shopping bags in and set them on the counter.

"Are you going to demand to put them away, too?" I tease.

I'm joking, but something tells me that if I weren't about to start baking right now and need the stuff out, he would demand it.

"No, because after I did all this work for you, I deserve the cookies I was promised."

"I don't remember promising you anything," I reply, the teasing sass still in my tone as I tilt my head and cross my arms, watching him take the items out of the bag.

"Really? Because this morning, after you got done moaning my name, I could have sworn I heard you promise to make me cookies for making you come so hard."

My mouth drops open as I try to contain my smile while I pick up a bag of Rolos off the counter and playfully throw it at him. "Watch me make them only to shove them up your ass."

"That's not the way I like to play, princess, but I'm down to be all over your ass." Logan winks at me as he crumples up the plastic bags.

My face is on fire at Logan's comment, leaving me speechless.

"Don't you have a fire to build?" I ask after a few moments, changing the subject.

"I'll build it if you get to baking. I'm hungry."

"Out." I point toward the living room.

"Don't burn your hand again." Are Logan's parting words as he leaves the kitchen.

Looking down at the wound from a few nights ago, I can't help but roll my eyes. The blister has gone down, and I don't think it's going to leave a scar, thank God.

I need a minute to breathe. Just when I think I'm holding my ground with him, he goes and says something to knock me off my axis. I'm not used to that. I always have the upper hand and am in control.

Not that it's a bad thing. I kind of like that Logan keeps me on my toes. It's refreshing. I haven't found myself bored at all with him.

It's easy.

Too fucking easy.

I spend the next few hours baking. I've made a couple dozen Rolo sugar cookies, shortbread cookies and my personal favorite, a Twix cookie.

It's not made from an actual candy bar, but somehow tastes exactly like you're eating one. It's safe to say I could eat my body weight in all of these.

With Logan's fire roaring and with the heat from the oven, the chill is completely gone from the cabin.

"Are they about ready?" Logan calls from the couch.

"Soon!" I reply as I carefully place the last of the cookies on the cooling rack, careful not to break any. "They need to cool down first!"

I hear Logan sigh as he turns and the volume on the T.V. turns up.

Good.

Now's the perfect time to wrap my gifts and put the stuff I brought with me under the tree.

I quickly clean up the kitchen and place the dishes on the drying rack to dry before heading toward the loft.

"I'm going to change into something comfy," I tell Logan as I pass him, heading straight for the stairs, hoping he doesn't follow me.

Luck is on my side because he stays where he is.

I quickly change into a pair of fuzzy lounge pants and a ribbed tank top before plopping my ass on the floor with Logan's ornament and flannel. I make quick work of wrapping them with the scraps of paper I brought with me just in case I needed a little extra.

I cringe to myself at my wrap job. It's a little patchy and honestly looks like a toddler wrapped them, but it's the thought that counts, right?

"You about ready?" Logan calls up. "I'm fucking starving and about two seconds away from starting without you!"

"You better not! The first cookie will be eaten at the start of the first movie!" I yell down to him as I put away my supplies and grab his gifts in my hand and jog down the stairs. "You can't mess with traditions."

"Traditions?" Logan's brow raises. "Did I miss your coming to my cabin every year?"

"No." I roll my eyes as I walk past him and head to the suitcase that's down here with the gifts for myself in it. "This is what I do every year. It doesn't matter where you're at as long as you're doing the same thing you love every year. That's what makes it a tradition."

I can feel Logan studying me from across the room.

"You going to let me in on all the traditions or just this one?" Logan asks after a long moment.

Am I?

There's a reason I bought him gifts. I could have easily let him watch me pathetically open up the gifts I bought myself and not have gotten him anything. It's not a lot, but I still felt the need to include him even though at the time I never expected to be where we are now.

Filling my arms with gifts from the suitcase, I make my way over to the tree and plop down in front of it.

"I'm letting you watch Christmas movies and eat my cookies, aren't I?" I finally answer Logan as I strategically place the gifts under the tree.

Larger gifts are in the back as I work my way to the smallest in the front.

"I'll give you that," Logan replies. "What Christmas movie did you want to start with?"

"The Holiday." My reply is instantaneous.

I could watch that movie every single day of the year for the rest of my life. Both of the love stories pull at my heartstrings for completely different reasons.

"You're going to have to find it, princess. The only Christmas movie I watch is A Christmas Story, and that's only because every channel thinks that's all they're allowed to play on Christmas." Logan tosses the remote. It lands on one of the gifts, creating a small tear in the paper.

He's not wrong.

By the time Christmas is over, I never want to watch that movie again.

My eyes are glued to where the remote fell. Slowly turning my head around so I'm looking at Logan, I shoot him a glare.

"Sorry." He smiles sheepishly, not sounding the least bit sorry.

My eyes narrow.

"Don't make me kick you out of Christmas movie night."

Logan lets out a loud laugh as he throws his head back. "You're going to kick me out of my own living room?"

"If you keep it up, yeah." I turn my attention back to arranging the presents under the tree because I can't keep the smile off my face to save my life.

"If you kick me out, then who are you going to cuddle with, huh?"

I freeze as I'm placing the last gift under the tree, front and center.

Cuddling?

That never even crossed my mind. After last night, I have zero doubts that he can't back up the game he talks, but I never pegged him as a cuddler.

"Someone who knows not to fuck up my work," I sass as I grab the remote and stand up.

"Who else did you have in mind?" Logan asks as I walk past him toward the kitchen, tossing the remote in his lap.

"I don't know." I shrug. "There has to be someone in town."

As I'm piling cookies on a plate, I sneak a glance at Logan, who is now angled in the corner of the couch with his arms resting on the back of the couch with his legs up on the coffee table. He's looking at me intently.

"What?" I ask, not quite understanding the blank look that's aimed right at me.

"You know what. You bring someone else into my cabin, not only will they have to answer to me, but you will too."

A chill runs down my spine from the promise in his voice.

"What would you do to me?"

"After I beat some ass, I'm going to throw you over my knee and spank your ass raw for you thinking it's okay to entertain someone else. I don't share."

The finality in his tone has me mindlessly grabbing the plate of cookies and sitting down next to him on the couch. Logan grabs the plate out of my hands and sets it down on the coffee table before he grabs my legs and pulls them into his lap.

My left brow raises as he throws a blanket over both of us.

"What?" he asks as he reaches over my legs to grab the plate of cookies off the table, balancing it on my legs.

"Where did you get a blanket?"

I looked all over this living room since I've gotten here, and I haven't once seen a throw blanket lying around.

"There's some in the closet upstairs." Logan grabs my foot, careful of the plate, and starts rubbing the arch of my foot.

My head falls back as a soft groan escapes my mouth.

Holy shit, that feels good.

"You going to put a movie on?"

Picking my head up, I grab the remote and turn on the T.V., clicking the streaming service I want and finding The Holiday.

"I know this goes without saying, but if there're any doubts, there shouldn't be. If I didn't like you, I wouldn't be watching chick flicks all night with you," Logan says, eyes on the screen as he pops a Twix cookie in his mouth. "Holy shit, that's good."

"They're not all chick flicks," I mumble, trying to keep the smile off my face at his admission.

"Right," Logan says sarcastically with a mouth full of cookie. "Let's see what this is all about."

I wiggle my butt, settling deeper into the couch as Logan continues to massage my foot. It's hard to focus on the movie when he's touching me in places I didn't even know would turn me on and relax me at the same time.

I think it's more about the intimacy of the moment. It's crazy that I'm able to be as comfortable around him as I am with my friends back home. All I can think about when the part in the

the movie where Cameron Diaz throws her boyfriend's stuff out of the window because he cheated on her was that Logan never would.

We aren't even close to the level of Cameron Diaz and her basically ex-boyfriend in the movie, but I feel more connected to him than that long-term relationship.

"It's my favorite," I whisper, not thinking he heard me as I grab a cookie off of the plate and take a small bite as I zone into the movie.

I can feel Logan's gaze on me, but I don't acknowledge it. I'm in the zone for the Christmas movie marathon.

Before I know it, the cookies are gone, and the credits are rolling on the screen.

"So let me get this straight," Logan starts as he readjusts on the couch, hiking my leg up further as he rests his hand on my calf, squeezing the muscle lightly. "They both fell in love with someone the person they swapped houses with knew?"

"Yup," I say excitedly. "Isn't it great? They both got their happy ending after being miserable for years."

"But they live in different countries."

"Didn't you see the ending scene? They were all together in one house for a holiday."

"So they moved to be with each other?"

My mouth opens and closes as I think about it. "I don't know," I exclaim. "But I feel like it's implied that everyone has a happily ever after."

I've always wondered what it would be like to find a love so powerful that you would do anything to keep it going, including moving to a new country. I'll never admit it out loud, but I've always been a hopeless romantic.

I've just given up after many failed dates and relationships that never seem to make it past the six-month mark. It's so goddamn exhausting going through the get to know you phase over and over again.

Logan's quiet for a moment as he studies me. "Would you do anything for your happily ever after?"

My breath gets caught in my throat at his question.

Would I?

I'd like to think I would, but it would come down to how I'm feeling about everything in my life, with and without that person.

"I think so…" I finally answer, trailing off as I was thinking about it. "If I were so stupid in love to the point where I feel like I'm so wrapped up in them that I can't breathe without them, then yeah, I would do whatever it takes to make it work."

Logan's assessing gaze hasn't wavered from me. "Have you ever felt like that before?"

Without counting now?

"No."

"You'll find it."

"I hope so," I softly reply as I turn my attention back to the T.V., scrolling through to find the next movie. "Have you ever felt like that before?"

I don't know what possessed me to ask him that. It came right out of my mouth like word vomit. All I know is I can't look at him when he answers, so I continue my pursuit of finding the next movie to watch as I anxiously wait.

He's older than I am.

I'd be a fool to think he's never had anyone in his life. And at his age, it's probably more of a 'the one that got away' type of love.

And for some crazy fucked up reason, hearing that would hurt.

"No," Logan finally answers. The hand that's massaging my calf tightens at the admission. "Tried to find her, but never did. I hoped I would by the time I turned forty, but it just wasn't in the cards for me."

I hate hearing the sadness he's trying to mask in his voice because this hardworking man deserves to have everything he wants out of life. But on the other hand, I'm probably going to hell for being so goddamn relieved he hasn't found it. I'd hate to have to hunt her down and shank a bitch on my way home for a peace of mind. It sounds like it would be a huge detour of inconvenience.

"So you what? Just gave up?" I'm proud of how well I'm hiding the fact that I'm happy he hasn't found her.

Logan runs a hand down his mouth as his eyes flash to me. "I wouldn't say I gave up. I just stopped looking. Some guys don't give a fuck, but for me there's only so many times I can take a woman out and have her not appreciate what I'm doing or they're only in it because of the money. And it's not that I don't want to take care of a woman like that because I do. I just want the reason she's with me to be that she loves me and what we have, not because of the fact that she would never have to work another day in her life if she didn't want to."

This time, I pause my search for a movie and turn my attention to Logan.

"So you think one day you'll find her? Like the universe will place her in your path when it feels you're ready?"

Logan releases a big sigh that has his chest visibly rising and falling. "Something like that."

"Well, for what it's worth, once she gets past your grumpy exterior, she'll realize you have a huge heart and would do anything to give her the world. I've known you for a little over a week and can already tell that. I've learned it doesn't matter how long you've known someone. When she's worth your appreciation, you'll know."

Logan is silent as he studies me, his face unreadable.

"I think I'll know too, princess."

CHAPTER
Fourteen

WYNN

The next few days are full of the same routine we've had, except something has shifted between us.

Instead of Logan sleeping on the couch every night, he's in bed with me. I don't know how it happened it just kind of did. After our movie night and talk, that turned deeper than either of us expected, he turned off the T.V. when I started dosing off, telling me to head upstairs and he'll be up in a minute.

I was thanking myself with every step that I only packed sexy pajamas, not that they were any use because each time Logan saw a new set, somehow it came off of me faster than I put it on.

During the day, we fell into a routine that felt comfortable. He still had to chop wood for the fireplace, but it wasn't at the ass crack of dawn like before. It's crazy to admit, but I've already gotten used to waking up with him holding me close, pressed up against his side with my head on his chest.

We haven't gone back into town since the last grocery trip, but I also haven't asked. It's a wild feeling to have when you're usually a person who needs to leave the house once a day or else you feel cooped up, but instead you feel the opposite because you have everything you need with the person you're with.

It's going to be a sad fucking day when I have to leave him behind.

I'm trying my best not to think about it, but it's hard not to when Christmas Eve is today, meaning I only have two days left.

"Are you sure you don't want to go back home and spend Christmas with your brothers?" I ask at the dining table during breakfast that morning.

I'm not eating, just sipping on some coffee I had to put ice in to make cold, but I made Logan eggs and bacon that he's currently devouring like he hasn't eaten in days.

I've never been a huge breakfast person. Partly because I'm never hungry in the morning and also because I'd rather wait and eat a larger lunch.

Logan pauses, bringing the next bite of food to his mouth, his fork hanging midair as he looks at me. "No. Do you want me to go back?"

No.

I would give anything to spend one Christmas with you.

"I don't want you to go back, but I also don't want you to miss out on spending a holiday with your family," I say quietly as I stare at the milky colored coffee in my cup as I trace the rim of the cup with my finger.

Logan's fork clatters on his plate, drawing my attention to him.

"What are you trying to say?" he asks.

"I just told you. I don't want you to feel like you have to stay here with me."

Logan's head rears back as the top corner of his lip raises. "I'm here because I want to be here. I told you my mom canceled Christmas this year, and my brothers aren't doing shit. If I had to pick between shitty Chinese food and video games all day with them or spending time with you, I'm going to pick you every time."

I can't do anything but stare at Logan. To be honest, I'm floored at his admission. I haven't met his brothers, but from what he's told me, I can tell it's a tight-knit family. And what guy doesn't like video games?

Clara constantly complains that Hudson is always playing games and never pays attention to her.

"Okay," I finally reply softly.

"Okay," Logan repeats, picking his fork back up and shoveling food onto it. "Where did that come from?"

"Where did what come from?" I ask, confused by his question.

Logan makes me wait until he's done chewing before answering. "You were soft and sweet for me this morning when I woke you up with my tongue. Not to mention the past few days, you've been extra sweet. Not once during that time did you question my not going home. So where did that come from?"

"I don't know." I sigh as I lean back in my chair. "I think I'm just getting into my own head. I've never had a relationship that was this easy before. It almost seems too good to be true. I don't know if that's also played up in my head, and by thinking about that, I kind of spiraled and just wanted to make sure you weren't staying here because you feel guilty I'm by myself or something."

"Relationship?" Logan asks, making my eyes widen.

Fuck.

"Um…" I trail off, trying to think of how I'm going to excuse my word vomit. "I didn't mean an actual relationship. Like a boyfriend or girlfriend type thing. I just meant a friendship. They're a type of relationship too."

Jesus Christ.

Can I sound any more cringe?

"You think we're just friends?"

"I… uh… yes?" It comes out sounding like a question because I honestly have no fucking clue what the correct answer is right now.

"Are you in the habit of fucking your friends?" Logan asks, his tone even, but I have a feeling if I answer wrong, it's not going to stay that way.

"No, I don't have a habit of fucking my friends," I answer softly.

I'm scared shitless right now.

The last thing I want to do is mess this up to the point of no return. He doesn't look uncomfortable, but Logan's always been good at not letting on how he's feeling. At this point, where this conversation goes is anyone's guess.

"Me neither." The chair creaks as Logan leans back, crossing his arms. "We're not just friends, princess. We crossed that line the second I sank my hard cock inside and your greedy cunt held on tight like it never wanted to let me go." My mouth drops open as he continues because, Jesus fucking Christ. I should be embarrassed, but I'm not. Instead, I'm turned on at the memory. "That doesn't give friends to me. What this is? I don't know. What

I do know is that I'll never be anyone's boyfriend, so get that out of your head."

"I… what?" I ask as I try to process everything he just said, but my brain can't keep up.

How can someone turn you on and confuse the hell out of you in the same breath?

"I'm too old to be anyone's boyfriend." I wasn't aware there was an age cap on something like that. "Judging by the look on your face, you're not following."

And I'm not.

I'm stuck on trying to figure out how my asking if he was sure he wanted to spend the holiday here led the conversation to him telling me he's too old to be anyone's boyfriend.

"I'm not asking you to be my boyfriend…" I say slowly, still very confused.

"I know you're not. And I wouldn't accept even if you were."

Oh.

The tightness in my chest is back, and it feels like my insides are slowly dying. I appreciate someone who can be blunt about their feelings, but damn it hurts coming from someone you could see having that title for the last time.

"Hey," Logan says softly, getting my attention. "Wipe that look off your face."

"What look?" I ask, trying my best to smile through the pain in my chest, but even I can feel it's wonky.

"Like someone just killed your puppy."

"I'm fine," I try again, this time sounding slightly more reassuring than the last, but we both know I'm still full of shit.

"You deserve everything you want out of life, Wynn. What you don't deserve is a boyfriend because you deserve a fucking man who is never going to leave your side."

Logan throws his crumpled up napkin on top of his empty plate at his admission before sliding his chair back and standing up, taking his plate to the sink while once again I sit in stunned silence.

I'm trying everything in my power not to get my hopes up in thinking Logan wants to claim that spot as his.

It would be extremely naive of me.

And yet here I am thinking it.

"What are your Christmas Eve traditions?" Logan asks, changing the subject.

I give him that because I'm in no shape to dig deeper into what he just laid out.

"I usually open up a gift and find Christmas lights to look at."

Crap.

I probably should have looked up to see if there is any sort of light show around here.

"We missed the walk downtown by about a month, but everyone around here has stuff up in their yard. We can drive around and find some."

My eyes widen as I watch Logan walk past me to put another log on the fire. "You want to go look at Christmas lights?"

"You want to go, don't you?"

"Yeah."

"Then I want to go too."

I shouldn't be shocked. Since his declaration at the bar, he's been glued to my hip.

"Alright," I say with a soft smile. "I can drive this time."

A loud laugh erupts from Logan. "I don't think so."

My eyes narrow. "Why not?" I ask with my hands on my hips.

"I'm not getting into that deathtrap you call a car."

"It's not a death trap!"

"How many times did you almost go into the ditch on your way here?"

My mouth opens and closes as I decide whether I should lie or not. I saw my life flash before my eyes enough times during that drive to last me the rest of my life, but I can't tell him that.

"Exactly." Logan gloats, reading my face. "Those aren't made for snow. Besides, I don't think I would fit into that car."

Hmm... he has a point there.

I sometimes feel cramped in it, which is crazy considering I'm not that tall. I've been thinking about trading it in. I'm just unsure of what to get.

"I think it would be fine if you pushed the seat all the way back," I argue.

I don't care how many valid points he's making. I refuse to let him win outright.

"I'm not pushing a seat all the way back to fit into a death trap. We're taking the truck."

"Can I drive your truck?" I ask, deciding to change my angle because he isn't budging.

"No."

"Why not?" I asked, shocked, and turned on at the same time that he told me no.

I was beginning to think he didn't have it in after the shift we had at the bar. He's been a yes-man ever since.

"As long as my ass is in a vehicle with you, I'm driving."

"So if you're not with me, I can drive your truck?"

"Sure."

"Is that a Michigan thing?"

Logan lets out another laugh as he looks at me like I'm crazy. "What? No, it's a man thing. No woman of mine is going to be driving me around. Makes me feel like a pussy."

Woman of mine?

I'm starting to think he isn't aware of what's coming out of his mouth, so I'm just going to leave it alone. As much as I want to ask what he meant by that, it's not something I want to get into on Christmas Eve.

I didn't expect to wake up missing my mom so much this morning, but I did. She's been gone for almost two decades now. You would think it would get easier, but in reality, it doesn't. You just learn how to live without them. The pain never really goes away.

Waking up with Logan's face between my thighs was a nice distraction, but it was short-lived. I would have stayed in bed all day with that man if I could have. Being close to him makes all the unhappy thoughts not seem so bad.

"Fine, you can drive." I roll my eyes as I give in.

Pushing my chair back, I get up and dump the last bit of my coffee in the sink.

"I was going to drive the whole time." Logan smirks at me as I join him in the living room on the couch.

"If I really wanted to, you would let me," I say, daring him to disagree with me.

The smirk that hasn't left his face lets me know I'm right, and that feels good. I like that he doesn't always cave and fights me along the way, but if it's something I truly want, he'd give in.

"If you were home with your family, what would you be doing?" I ask as I tuck my feet under myself.

Logan leans back against the cushions, stretching an arm across the back in what I've come to learn is how he always sits on the couch.

"Christmas Eve isn't huge for us. We all kind of do our own thing during the day and then come together at night for dinner, which is more appetizers than anything and drinks. Lots and lots of drinks. If we aren't a little hungover on Christmas, then we didn't do it right."

"That sounds fun." I smile. "I have so many random appetizers and small plates saved on my phone that I've found online, but making them all seems silly when it's just me. Cooking for one blows. I make either not enough for one meal or enough to feed twenty people. There's no in-between."

"It does suck, doesn't it?" Logan says, his attention on me. But then again, his attention is always on me when I'm talking to him. He never makes me feel like he'd rather be anywhere but with me. "I pretty much stopped cooking and just pop in to my parents' house for dinner. Mom always makes enough to feed everyone."

"You drive over to your mom's house every night?" I ask, trying to figure out their dynamic.

"It's just up the lane. Usually, I just take the gator."

"Up the lane?"

"We all live on the same piece of land, princess. My dad gave us each our own lot, and my brothers and I built our own houses on it."

Huh.

That actually would be kind of cool. Kind of like your own family compound.

"I can see the wheels turning, and before you spiral, no, I'm not so attached to my parents that I can't leave the nest. The houses aren't on top of each other. It just made sense since we all work on the farm."

I feel the need to slide closer to Logan because I don't want him to think I thought it was weird they all live so close, so I do.

Scooching my butt over until our knees are touching and I can rest my hand on his upper thigh, I say, "I'm not judging you. I think it's cool that you're so close to your family. Not many people have that. And who cares if you all live on the same piece of land? It's not like you're forty years old living in your parents' basement. If that were the case, this would be a different conversation."

Logan's body relaxes beneath my touch as he places his hand on top of mine, lightly tracing my fingers with his.

"Has that been an issue in the past?" I push, sensing there is more to this than what he's letting on.

"Some women haven't been as... happy to see another woman involved in my day-to-day life."

"But it's your mom?" I ask, confused.

Am I missing something here?

She doesn't sound overbearing or so in his life that she's making his every move. The fact that she canceled Christmas alone tells me she isn't like that.

"I know." He shrugs. "There wasn't much I could do about it. I'm willing to do a lot for someone I love, but cutting out my family when I know they're good people isn't one of them."

I look at him. And I mean really look at him.

And while I'm looking at him, all I can think about is how cruel the universe is for placing someone with the qualities that make up my dream guy so far away.

"Don't ever change, big guy," I tell him before picking up the remote and turning on a Christmas movie to pass the time until it's time to go look at lights.

CHAPTER
Fifteen

WYNN

"Y ou about ready to go?" Logan yells from downstairs.

I just finished the final touches on my hair and makeup and am now doing one last once-over in the mirror to make sure everything looks semi-decent.

Originally, when I thought I was going by myself, I was just going to throw on some leggings and a hoodie and call it a day. No one would see what's under my coat if I got out of my car, anyway.

But when I found out Logan was going to go with me?

Absolutely not.

I'm going to be in the delusional part of my head where he and I are actually together and this is a date. When I'm back home in Virginia, I want to look back on this trip and know I gave it my all, and each moment was perfect, even if it was just a vacation fling.

I know when I pack my car up and pull out of this driveway, I will not be okay.

I probably won't be okay for a long time, if ever.

It's going to be hell not comparing every single guy I meet after this to Logan.

"Almost!" I yell back.

Throwing my fur coat over my arm, I jog down the stairs with my boots in hand.

"Sorry it took so long," I say, giving him an apologetic smile.

"I didn't know what to wear."

An amused look takes over Logan's face. "We're just going to drive around and look at Christmas lights, princess. You could have worn sweatpants if you wanted to." I open my mouth to defend myself, but Logan prowls on. "But for future reference, I'll wait for you any time of the day for any length of time because every single time I've waited on you since you barged into my life, it's been worth it."

My belly swirls as I stare at him, boots and coat still in my arms and hand.

How in the hell is this man single?

"Well, either way, I'll try to make sure it doesn't happen again."

"Do I look mad?"

"No."

"You look gorgeous, Wynn." Logan's eyes are locked on mine, the sincerity in his words shining bright. "You ready to go see some lights?"

"Yeah," I exclaim excitedly.

Logan opens the front door, waits for me to walk through it before closing it and locking up. Taking my hand in his, we walk to his truck together, which he already had running, so it's warm for me.

"We're going to a zoo?" I ask as Logan turns into the entrance for one.

I love his enthusiasm for being up for doing anything that I want to do, but I've never heard of zoos being open at night for animal viewing, let alone when it's this cold out.

"When you were getting ready, I searched on the internet if there were any light displays in the area, and this came up. None of the animals are out, but they opened up the park and turned it into a drive-through light display."

My belly is doing that swirling thing it did earlier from all the sweet things Logan keeps throwing my way.

It's like just when I think he can't top it, he goes and does something like this.

"You didn't have to do that," I whisper, unable to keep the huge smile off my face as I can see the park lit up with colorful lights off in the distance.

"I wanted to." Logan's free hand that isn't on the wheel moves to rest on my upper thigh, giving it a light squeeze before leaving it in what's becoming his signature spot.

Logan rolls down the window as he slows to a stop at the pay booth.

"Merry Christmas!" the girl dressed head to toe in Carhartt overalls and a jacket greets as she steps out from the booth. "How many people do we have in the car tonight? Five get in for a single vehicle charge."

"Just us," Logan's deep voice rumbles, making the inside of my thighs tingle.

"Perfect!" she exclaims in the same high-pitched, cheerful voice. "It'll be twenty-five dollars!"

Without removing his hand from my thigh, Logan leans over onto one hip and pulls his wallet out of his back pocket with his other hand. Flipping it open, he pulls out his card and hands it over.

A simple move shouldn't turn me on so much, but it does.

God, it fucking does.

At this point, Logan could breathe, and I would think it's hot.

"There's that back for you." She hands Logan his card back. "Just follow the path! It's a one way and you'll end back around here, coming out on the other side over there," she continues as she points to the road on the other side of the booth. "The only thing we ask is that you try to keep the speed under ten miles per hour and watch out for stopped vehicles. Some of the displays are animated and take a few minutes to play out entirely, so folks like to stop and watch the show. There is themed music to go along with your ride. If you would like to listen, just turn your radio to 87.5 FM! Any questions?"

My own cheeks hurt from watching her do her spiel with that massive smile on her face that hasn't left the entire time.

"Nope," Logan answers for us. "I think we're good. Thanks."

"Perfect! You two enjoy the show now!" She steps back from the truck, retreating to her booth as Logan pulls away, rolling up his window.

He pulls off to the side, his hand refusing to leave my thigh as he turns the radio to the station she told us, and sure enough, Christmas music starts playing.

"That girl was…" I trail off, not wanting to sound like a complete asshole but also needing to voice my shock at how someone could really act like that. It's like they plucked her right out of a Hallmark movie and stuck her in Northern Michigan.

"A lot?" Logan finishes with a laugh.

"Yes," I join him. "I didn't know someone could be so… much."

"That's one way of fucking putting it. Do me a favor, princess, and reach into the back and grab that cooler."

Shooting Logan a side glance, I do what he asks.

My hand blindly searches until I feel the handle. Grabbing it, I heave it up onto the center console.

Was I so far into my own head when we walked out of the cabin that I didn't realize he was carrying a cooler?

"Open it up," Logan demands, and, well, who am I not to give the man what he wants?

Pushing the little circle on the side, I pull the top down to reveal a thermos and two mugs.

My confused gaze shoots up to Logan, who is looking pretty smug with himself right now.

"You can't go looking at Christmas lights without some hot cocoa."

This time, my belly swirls almost enough to make my heart stop.

"You did this for me?" I barely got out. I'm not even sure if he heard me; my voice is so soft.

"I'd do anything to put a smile on your face, baby. Open it up and pour us a glass so we can get this show on the road."

My head hasn't caught up with my body as it starts going through the motions of pouring us a glass of hot cocoa and even puts marshmallows in it. Fucking marshmallows.

"This is the sweetest thing anyone has ever done for me," I tell him, needing to get that out because a gesture like this shouldn't go unappreciated even if, to most people, it's small.

Logan doesn't say anything as he squeezes my thigh before pulling onto the small road to start the light show.

The light show was everything I wanted it to be. I oohed and aahed at almost every display, even gasping at some.

I don't know how they did it, but some of the displays were timed up with the radio station and played a song for that set.

It was so goddamn cool.

Before meeting Logan, I would have been cringing so hard at how I'm being. This whole adventure that started out as a trip in memory of my mom by doing all the things she wanted somehow turned out to be something magical for me.

I'd like to think it would have been that way on my own, but I'm not so sure it would have.

Not once did Logan get annoyed when I would grab onto his upper arm in excitement as I told him to look as if he wasn't already looking. Sometimes he wasn't. I could feel his attention on me more than the lights, and I loved that. Every time I looked over at him, he had this soft look on his face that I'd never seen before.

This has been one of the best nights of my life, and all we did was drive around and drink hot cocoa. He even brought a tumbler full of ice so I could drink it cold. I'm realizing it's not about what you do in life but more about who you do it with.

"Well?" I ask Logan as we exit the park.

"Well, what?" he asks, casting me a side glance but not taking his eyes fully off the road.

"You know damn well what I'm asking." I laugh, rolling my eyes at him. Don't think I didn't miss his little smirk. "Did you like it?"

"They were lights." He shrugs.

My laughter dies as my face evens out, the excitement I was feeling slowly dying. "You didn't like it."

"Princess, it isn't the lights I liked. It's the woman sitting next to me in my truck that I liked."

"You're laying it on thick, big guy. You can say you liked it. I won't tell anyone in case you're worried it will threaten your manhood," I tease even though inside I'm freaking the fuck out.

He's making it harder and harder not to blur the lines between what I have going on in my head and reality.

Logan's laugh booms throughout the truck. "It's not laying it on thick when it's true. And you don't need to worry about my manhood. Everyone thinks it's just fine. You screaming my name every single time I get up in there should tell you it's just fine."

I'm thankful it's dark out and he can't see how red my face is.

"I'm not that loud," I mumble to the window.

God, I really hope he's exaggerating.

"Princess, if the neighbors were any closer, they would hear you inside their cabin."

"Oh God," I groan as I cover my face with my hands.

How fucking humiliating.

"There's nothing to be embarrassed about. I like it. Makes me go harder." Logan's hand leaves my thigh and grabs my wrist, tugging my hand away from my face. "You don't ever need to be embarrassed about it. That's you and me. You might be a princess, but you're not a pillow princess, and I fucking love that."

I can't deny that being a pillow princess does have its appeal. Who wouldn't want to just lie there every once in a while and do nothing while they have an amazing orgasm?

Logan shoots me a knowing glance. "If you want to lie there and take it, baby, go on ahead. You know I'm always hungry."

Jesus, this fucking man.

"Is there anything else you want to do tonight while we're out?" Logan asks as he heads back toward town. "I don't know if there's much open with it being late and Christmas Eve and all."

"Not really," I tell him as I try to think if there's anything else. "The only other thing I want to do is open one gift."

"I'll get you a nice fire going, and I'll watch you open up your gift, princess." Logan's hand is back on my thigh, only this time stroking up and down, making desire bloom between my legs. I'm hot all over, but it isn't from the heat blasting through the vents.

It's from him.

I just hope he likes my gift.

CHAPTER
Sixteen

WYNN

A s soon as we got back to the cabin, I bolted upstairs to change into Logan's first gift, the one he will open tonight, using the excuse that I want to be comfortable while he gets the fire going.

I'm trying to swallow the bundle of nerves that are working their way up my throat begging me to back out, but if there's one thing my mom did while she was alive, she made sure she didn't raise a bitch. Well, she did, but not a chicken shit kind of bitch.

Grabbing the shopping bag I hid, I pull out the black and red flannel lingerie set. I quickly dart to the bathroom and slip inside and quietly shut the door.

I make quick work of stripping out of my clothes. Popping the tags off, I say a silent prayer that this fits and will look as good as it does in my head because God knows when you plan an outfit like that you end up looking like straight trash. I'm kicking myself for not trying this on sooner.

I know Logan would take me anyway I come, but I want this to work so goddamn bad.

Slipping on the red and black flannel thong with black lace trim, I say a silent thank you as it fits like a glove. The bustier bra fits as if it were made for me. After adjusting myself, the girls are spilling out over top slightly but not in a trashy way. Stepping into the high black lace suspenders with accompanying attached lace garters, I fully look at myself in the mirror.

I look fucking hot.

It looks like I cut up Logan's signature flannel shirt, added lace, and made myself into a sexy lumberjack vixen.

Topping this with a pair of baggy sweatpants and a T-shirt, I trot back downstairs just as I hear a cork pop off a bottle of wine.

My eyes search out Logan, finding him in the living room with two glasses and a bottle of red.

"The lumberjack is having wine?" I ask, unable to keep the shock out of my voice.

I've had a few glasses since I've been here and never once have I seen him drink anything other than the shitty Natural Light.

"Don't look so shocked. I drink it from time to time." Logan pours us each a glass before setting the bottle down on the coffee table. "And this seemed like a good time."

Logan assumes his usual position on the couch as my eyes roam his body.

He's in his Levi's that were made to fit him and his body alone, a tight white undershirt and the black and red flannel with the top two buttons undone. His left arm is thrown lazily over the back of the couch as his right hand is dangling the wine glass, his assessing gaze aimed right at me.

"You going to open up your present, princess?" he asks, his voice coming out gravelly as he brings the glass to his lips, taking a small sip, his eyes never leaving me.

"Yes." I swallow.

The way he's looking at me feels like a promise of what's coming later and makes my body feel like it's on fire.

Grabbing my wine glass, I chug half of it before setting it back down and making my way over to the tree to grab a gift, needing something to settle my nerves.

"Do you remember what's in everything you wrapped?" Logan asks as I sit down next to him.

"Not really." I smile sheepishly. "I've been planning this trip since last Christmas, so throughout the year I slowly bought stuff I thought I would like to open. It's stupid, I know."

"It's not stupid. I buy shit for myself all the time. The only difference is you're wrapping yours, and I used mine immediately."

I guess when he puts it like that, he's right.

"The suspense is killing me."

My eyes lift up to Logan, who is watching me intently with a smile on his face. The only thing that's stopping me from feeling guilty about opening something up in front of him when he has nothing is this little number I have on underneath my clothes.

"Didn't your mom ever tell you that good things come to those who wait?"

Logan's lip tips up. "Once or twice. Doesn't mean I listened."

My eyes roll as I rip a corner of the paper off.

Typical male, never fucking listening.

Ripping the rest of the paper off, I gasp at the new e-reader in my hand.

"Did you honestly forget what you bought yourself?" Logan's laughing so hard that he's shaking the couch.

"I may have a small shopping problem," I mumble as I set it down on the couch next to me. "Did your mom at least get you any gifts?"

If she doesn't then she really means business about wanting them all to settle down. I don't think I've ever heard of someone going to such extremes to get it, though.

"I doubt it. Knowing her, she's just trying to make a point. When she and my dad get back from their trip, she'll have something for all of us."

"That's good. I'd hate for you to have nothing."

Don't give it away.

"Why are you looking at me like that?"

"Like what?" I ask, unaware of how I was looking at him.

"Like you know something that I don't."

"I don't know." I shrug, trying to play it off without giving anything away. I've always been a shitty liar. "I probably know a lot of things you don't."

Logan throws his head back, letting out a belly laugh. "If it involves a fur coat, then yeah, princess, you know more than me." Logan leans forward and nabs my glass off the table. "Drink up so I can top us off. I have another bottle I want to open tonight."

My brow shoots up. "Specifically for tonight?"

"Got it a while ago when my mom dragged us to a winery up north. The lady there said it was one of their best runs of it."

Emotion starts to swirl in my belly again as my chest grows tight. "Are you sure you want to open it tonight and not save it for something special?"

"Who said tonight isn't something special?"

Holy shit.

I'm unable to form a coherent sentence, but good thing my body has a mind of its own because before I know it, I've downed the rest of the wine in my glass and Logan is popping up the next bottle.

"It's good," I tell him after taking a small sip.

"You looked beautiful tonight, Wynn," Logan says, ignoring me completely.

"Thank you," I whisper.

The heat in his eyes is igniting a burning need in my body that's working its way between my legs. They hold an unfilled promise of what he's been hinting at all night long.

"Come here, Wynn." The fire cracks and pops after Logan's rumble, sending a shiver down my spine.

I scooch closer to him until our thighs are touching.

His hand comes up, cupping the side of my face as his thumb softly strokes behind my ear.

"Did you have a good Christmas Eve?" His face is now inches from mine, his warm breath tickling my skin.

"I did. Thank you." My lids lower to his mouth.

Part of me wants to lean in the last couple of inches and close the gap, but I've come to know Logan by now, and I know that would be the wrong move. He's in control.

Logan doesn't leave me waiting as he touches his lips to mine in a closed-mouth kiss. It's soft at first, but like everything seems to be with us, it goes from zero to one hundred in three seconds.

There's no exploring and working up to it. Its pure dominance. Logan is taking what's his, whether he knows it or not.

Without breaking the kiss, Logan pulls me into his lap so I'm now straddling him, his hard cock pressing into my thigh through his jeans. Instinctively, I grind my hips down, wanting to feel him everywhere. A long groan escapes his lips, my mouth drowning it out.

Logan places his hands under my ass and slides forward on the couch, taking me with him as he moves to stand up.

I tear my lips away, leaning forward against his as I try to catch my breath. I'd be embarrassed by how turned on I am right now if Logan wasn't breathing equally hard.

Logan walks toward the fireplace and drops to his knees, making me let out a squeal from the unexpected move.

"What—"

"Ever since I saw you in that fucking fur coat of yours, I couldn't stop thinking about having you on the fur rug," Logan says, his voice gravely as he lowers me to the floor. "Yeah," he rumbles. "My princess looks fucking delicious in fur."

Holy.

Fucking.

Shit.

Did I die and go to heaven?

A surge of wetness floods my already damp panties from the dirty words coming out of this man's mouth.

Logan looms over me as his hand slides under the hem of my shirt, moving up to caress my side. He pauses when he feels the lace belt around my waist holding up the suspenders, his lids lifting to mine.

"What do you have on under here?" Logan asks, his brow lowering as he removes his hand and grabs the hem of my baggy T-shirt. I have no choice but to lift off the floor slightly as he pulls it over my head. His swift intake of breath can be heard throughout the room before a low growl rumbles out of his chest. "Holy shit."

"Merry Christmas, big guy," I say, my tone sultry as a seductive smirk spreads across my lips. "We match."

Logan's mouth parts in shock. "Please tell me there are matching panties."

"Why don't you take the rest off and find out for yourself?"

Logan wastes no time pulling my sweatpants down my legs, revealing the matching thong and the black lace garters.

"Fuck," he groans as his large hands land on my knees and start rubbing their way up my thighs. "You're like my fantasy woman come to life."

I squirm under Logan's heated gaze that's roaming my body, silently begging for any sort of contact.

"Are you going to stare at me all night or are you going to unwrap your fantasy?" I ask, sassily cocking a brow at him.

The wolfish grin Logan flashes me doesn't prepare for what happens next.

His hands roughly open my legs, wrapping them around him before he dives face first into my soaking wet pussy. Using a finger to slide the little piece of fabric to the side, his tongue gets down to business.

"Oh my God." I gasp, my hand slamming down on the top of his head, holding him in place.

The growl he lets out vibrates in all the right places, making me arch my hips and push his face deeper.

The welcoming tingle is burning. It's so close I can taste it.

His tongue laps my clit, faster and faster until I'm teetering on the edge, ready to fall over at any given moment. Without warning, Logan inserts two fingers as his tongue swirls. My head arches back as my orgasm washes over me, leaving me panting.

It's not enough.

It's never enough when it comes to him.

ogan pushes against my palm, which is still holding him in place as he comes up. His hungry gaze is eating me alive, but all I can focus on is my juices soaking the stubble that's shadowing his face.

Both of us are in a standoff and unmoving as our chests rapidly rise and fall.

Fuck waiting for him to make a move.

I dive forward, sticking my hands in the top of his shirt where the two buttons are undone and yanking the sides open. Buttons scatter all around us as his shirt falls open.

I yank it off his shoulders, desperate to get his undershirt off and feel his body heat on me.

"I love the set, princess. I really do, but tell me how I get it fucking off." One of his hands is working on the clasp at my back, and the other is trying to pull the belt over my hips and failing miserably. His eyes are roaming over me frantically, the desperation shining bright at not knowing where to start first.

I hear him talking, but I don't register what he's saying. I'm too busy trying to get the Levi's that are morphed to his body over his tight ass.

"What?" I ask, sounding as breathless and needy as I feel.

"Help me get this fucking thing off." Logan pulls the band of the bra back and lets go, letting it snap against my skin.

Moving to sit up, I reach around and unclip the hooks in record time before sliding the straps down my arms, my breasts spilling out as the cups fall to the ground.

Logan swiftly inhales before swooping in, taking a taunt bud in his mouth and lapping it with his tongue, nipping lightly along the way. I have to grab onto his shoulders to steady myself as my head falls back, and a gasp leaves my lips.

"Pants. Off. Now." I barely get out as I push on his shoulders.

I don't want his mouth to leave me, but I need him inside me or else I'm going to explode.

Logan hears the desperation in my voice and releases the bud with a pop. Cool air hits it, sending a shiver down my spine. He pulls his jeans and boxers off in one swoop, his hard cock bobbing as it springs free. Precum is leaking from the head, practically begging me to have a taste.

Unable to resist the urge, I lean down and lick the drop that's trailing down on the big head with a slow flick of my tongue. His cock jumps at the contact.

"Not too much of that." A hoarse laugh escapes Logan as he slides his hands around me and pulls me up so I'm sitting in his lap. My thighs press into his sides, and my forehead falls against his as he gropes my other breast. "The perfect handful," he softly groans, his breath tickling my lips.

Grinding down, his throbbing cock slips between my wet folds, making both of us moan.

Logan's lids lift to mine, matching my own that I know are heavy with need. The fire cracks and pops in the background as I lift just enough to wrap my hand around him and guide him to the place both of us desperately want.

I sigh into his neck as I slowly sink down onto him. It's still a tight fit, and the stretch of him brings a welcoming pinch I'm beginning to crave.

I'm an addict.

An addict for Logan's dick.

"I'll never get sick of feeling your tight pussy wrap me up, princess."

I mumble an incoherent agreement, too caught up in everything that's Logan.

Lifting my hips until just the head is in, I slide back down, taking the rest of him inside until I bottom out and can feel his balls against my ass.

I whimper into his neck as his cock pulses, making my walls flutter around him.

"I need you to move, baby. I'm dying here." Lifting my head up, I see Logan biting his bottom lip with his teeth as the veins in his neck are bulging out.

Who am I not to give the man what he wants most?

Slowly, I glide up and down his cock, crying out from the feel of him at this angle. He's deeper than he's ever been before. Logan's hands grab my hips, guiding me. I can feel his grunts and groans in my core, making my walls tighten around him.

"Jesus Christ," Logan growls at the same time I cry out as he hits that perfect spot just right, sending a rush of wetness coating his cock.

One of his hands cradles the back of my head as the other moves to my back as he lowers me to the rug, never losing contact. My eyes close as I let out a sigh from the feel of the soft fur of the rug against my back is sending my senses into overdrive.

"Look at me," he demands as he looms over me, thrusting in hard until he's to the hilt. My lids flutter open as I'm greeted by his hungry gaze. But that's not all I see. If I had the guts to call him on it, I swear its hungry adoration. "Wrap me up, Wynn."

On command, my legs wrap around his waist, and my arms loop around his neck, pulling him down to my lips. Logan sets a steady pace. It's not fast, but it's not slow. It's the perfect pace that's sending tears to my eyes from the emotion that's washing over me.

"Yeah," he grunts. "You feel it."

Still unable to form a sentence, all I can do is nod my head against his lips that are pressed to mine. Not in a kiss, though, no. This is about the connection and just being. No one has ever made love to me before, but this sure feels like it.

It's messy, and it's raw, but it's us.

My whimpers and moans are getting louder as he picks up the pace. My inner walls are flexing around him, alternating between a flutter and clamping him in a vice grip. I'm so fucking close.

Logan's hand sneaks between us as he presses a thumb to my clit. His tongue plunges into my mouth as I take him over the edge with me. I swallow his groan, and he swallows my scream.

He collapses on top of me, and I welcome his weight. My hands that were looped around his neck lightly trail up and down his spine, dragging my nails as I go in little scratches.

"You have to be the best thing that broke into my cabin," Logan rumbles in my ear, his voice still gravely as his softening dick slips out.

I playfully smack his back. "Shut up. I swear, if you continue to tell this story when you're 90 years old, I'm going to shove something up your ass."

"As long as you do it in your fur coat." Logan's body shakes with laughter on top of me before he rolls off to the side.

"I can't stand you," I sass, with no real meaning behind it.

"Seems like you like me just fine, princess."

I turn my head to the side and see Logan with his head propped up in his hand, smiling softly at me.

The last sheet of denial cracked inside my head, sending me tumbling face first into the realization that this isn't just some fantasy I've been living out in my head.

I'm in love with Logan Warner.

"Yeah, I guess I do."

CHAPTER
Seventeen

WYNN

I wake up the next morning with a sense of dread that's hanging over my excitement of it finally being Christmas.

Inside, I'm screaming as I jump up and down that Logan actually stayed. Part of me was so sure he would have driven home at least to spend the holiday with his brothers even if there would not be an actual celebration. It's his own blood, after all.

My jaw clenches as a bitter taste coats my tongue at the thought of having to pack up my tiny car and leave tomorrow. Which makes today my last day.

My last day with him.

I'm doing everything in my power not to think about it, but damn, it's hard.

Never in my life did I expect to fall in love in Northern Michigan, let alone so quickly. Everyone always told me when you know, you know, but why did it have to happen like this for me? Sometimes I think the universe hates me.

"Merry Christmas, princess." Logan places a soft kiss on my shoulder blade.

My heart flutters, and my belly does a little swoosh. I burrow back into him, welcoming the warmth of his embrace. His arm tightens around my waist, pulling me in tight.

"Merry Christmas, big guy," I reply softly, trying my best to keep the sadness out of my voice.

"Hey," Logan says just as softly as he squeezes me to him. "Why do you sound so sad? It's finally time for you to open all of your gifts."

I'm battling an internal war on whether I should come clean and tell him how I'm really feeling or make up a lie and try to play it off the best I can when inside I'm slowly dying.

The latter wins.

Sort of.

"I'm just thinking about how I wish my mom was here," I half-lie. I feel bad about not telling him what's really going on, but I don't want it to cloud the day for him too.

Logan places a soft kiss at the base of my neck. "She may not be here physically, but she's always with you. You're doing a damn good job of carrying on her memory."

"Yeah," I murmur. "I guess I am."

The air hangs heavy between us, neither of us willing to give voice to what tomorrow holds. His hand drifts in a slow caress along my side, while mine idly sketches patterns on the arm he's stretched beneath my pillow.

"You want to get up and get around, and I'll make you breakfast?"

"No," I reply, placing a kiss on his forearm.

"No?" Logan echoes.

"Christmas is the day when you get to stay in your pajamas without judgment as you open gifts and binge snacks."

"Is that what you and your mom did?" Logan asks as he takes a strand of my loose hair and twirls it around his finger.

"No." I laugh. "It's what I do because I'm usually by myself."

Logan tugs on my hair. "You aren't alone this year."

"I know, but that doesn't mean that tradition needs to change. I'd much rather snack all day long than eat a meal that's going to make me feel like I'm about to explode. Are you saying you don't want to partake?"

Logan's hand grips my chin, turning my head toward him. "Did I fucking say that?"

"No." I smirk, nipping his chin, shivering at the feel of his stubbly beard poking my face as I rub up against him.

A rumble vibrates his chest. "She gave me the best orgasm I've ever had in my life and is already ready for more."

My heart pounds in my chest at his admission.

Rolling over in his arms so I'm facing him. "The best orgasm of your life?"

Logan's brows raise. "If you try to tell me you didn't feel what I felt last night, I'm going to spank your ass raw."

I suck in a breath.

So he did feel it.

Do I do bitch out and act like I don't know what he's talking about since I'm leaving tomorrow, or do I admit that I'm pretty positive I'm in love with his stupid ass?

"No," I softly reply to his chest, unable to meet his eye. "I felt it."

God.

Why does he make me like this? I'm never embarrassed to say how I feel. I'm usually the first person to tell someone to fuck off or the first one to say out loud what everyone is thinking.

It's different with Logan.

For once, I'm actually scared of the rejection.

"Good." He places a soft kiss on my lips. "Let's head downstairs and start this day. I'm excited to experience a Wynn Christmas."

Logan releases my hand, tossing the covers aside as he heads for the bathroom, leaving me gaping after him, my eyes fixed on his retreating back. Good?

That's it?

Fucking good?

Well, fuck you too then, big guy.

I wish I could say that to his face.

I mean, I could. And I probably should. But do I really want to make the last day with him weird and probably ruin this memory?

Not really.

I'm going to take a loss on this one. I'm sure I'll be an out-of-character sobbing mess on my way home since I'm about to experience my first true heartbreak, but I'll eventually move on.

That's the one thing I'm good at.

Moving on.

Pushing through the pain like it never happened.

I hear the toilet flush in the bathroom and the sink turn on before the bathroom door opens, revealing a bare-chested Logan in gray sweatpants.

The same outfit he had been wearing the first night I met him. The deep V leading to what is becoming my favorite part about him has my eyes trailing down his body and finding it resting proudly against his thigh. He wore me out last night, but all I can think about is following the line it's created with my tongue.

"Are you just going to stare at me all day or are you going to get your ass out of bed and come downstairs and watch me make you breakfast?" Logan asks, leaning against the doorway with his arms crossed and a hip cocked. I can't hide the fact that I'm checking him out; his slightly raised lip shows he noticed.

Busted.

"Are you going to put a shirt on?"

"Wasn't planning on it. You ruined my favorite flannel last night."

Oops.

"Sorry." I shrug, not feeling the least bit sorry. "I'll watch you in the kitchen."

"I figured." Logan rolls his eyes, but the smile doesn't leave his lips. "Let's go, princess."

Throwing the covers off myself, I shiver as the cold air hits my skin. The fire must have died down during the night. I quickly put on a pair of lounge clothes and follow Logan downstairs.

A slow smile spreads across my face as I look out the window. Snow is falling down in giant, fluffy chunks. The kind of flakes you want to stick your tongue out for so you can catch them.

Logan is banging around in the kitchen as I head over to the tree and plug it in. The bright white lights fill up the room, making it feel as cozy as I pictured it would be in my head when I booked the listing.

"The tree looks good," Logan says as he shocks me by handing me an iced coffee. "I'll get the fire going so you stop shaking like a leaf, and then I'll make us some food. What?" he asks, taking in the look on my face.

"I didn't know you knew how to make an iced coffee." It's not like this place is up to date with appliances. I'm still surprised the ones he has still work.

"It's not rocket science. Are you going to drink it or not?"

I take the cup from his hands and sit down on the couch, but not without shooting him a glare before pulling a blanket over my lap. "Thank you."

I sip my coffee, closing my eyes and letting out a sigh as the caffeine hits my system.

I needed this.

Doors are opening and closing, almost as if he has no idea where anything is. But soon, the delicious smells of whatever he's making assault my nose, making my stomach rumble.

It isn't much longer before he's holding a plate full of eggs, toast and bacon in front of my face.

My eyes go from the plate to him, not expecting this but also expecting this at the same time.

"Are we really going to do this again?" he asks, his arm still outstretched.

I smile as I take the plate. "No." I just wasn't expecting the most basic breakfast known to man, but I guess this checks out for a guy like him. "Thanks for breakfast."

"You're welcome," Logan says as he sits down with a piece of toast in his mouth. "This is about the best I can do."

I snort. "Well, I'm sorry to say you won't be winning any awards soon but it's good."

"That's what I was going for."

Turning my head, I smile at Logan. His eyes zero in on the corner of my lip. Setting his fork down, he lifts his hand to my mouth and uses his thumb to wipe the corner of it.

Instinctively, I reach for the sheet of paper towel he gave me under my plate to use as a napkin.

"Just a little egg yolk," Logan murmurs as his tongue darts out, licking the tiny speck of yolk he wiped off me.

My body flushes at watching the tip of his tongue lap up something that came from my body, and my heart speeds up from the way he's looking at me.

"I'm ready," Logan says as he sets his plate down, breaking the moment, but the look on his face hasn't changed.

"Ready for what?"

If he says to fuck me, I swear I'll drop to my knees right now.

"To watch you open up all that shit." Logan's hand waves to the tree.

Oh.

Rolling my eyes, I set my plate down on the coffee table. I grab two presents, handing one off to Logan.

"What's this?" Logan asks as he studies the bag.

"It's nothing big. But you needed something to open on Christmas too," I say softly, unable to meet his eye.

I'm being the chicken shit I know my mom would hate right now because I don't have the guts to see his reaction.

"You didn't need to get me anything, Wynn. Thank you." I feel all fuzzy inside from the sincerity ringing in his voice.

The fuzzy feeling quickly turns to jittery nerves as I watch him pull pieces of tissue paper from the bag until he sees the first gift. Pulling it out, he carefully unwraps the paper, revealing the flannel I got him.

"To replace the one I ruined last night," I tell him as he traces the collar with his finger, a low smile spreading onto his lips.

"My favorite flannel being ruined will be a moment I'll never forget. Especially now that the woman who ruined it got my replacement." Logan winks, setting the shirt and bag down. "Come here."

I want nothing more than to jump into his outstretched arms, but I need him to open the last thing before I really chicken out. "There's something else in the bag."

Logan's brow lowers in question as he picks the bag back up and sticks his hand in as he fishes around before pulling out the gift Norma wrapped.

"What is it?" Logan asks as he turns it over.

"I don't know. Why don't you open it?" I return, trying to keep the nervousness out of my voice.

Logan makes quick work of unwrapping, revealing the gnome ornament with Wynn and Logan written under their respective gnome. The longer he goes without saying a word and stares at the ornament, the more I start to freak out inside.

I knew this was a bad idea.

It's not only corny, but who gets a man a Christmas ornament like that?

I'm about to throw Norma under the bus so hard for talking me into this.

"You had this made?" Logan's voice is quiet as his thumb runs over the gnomes.

"I wouldn't say I had it made. I mean, yeah, I had the names put on it, but the ornament itself was already done. I didn't request it or anything like that," I ramble, unsure of how to talk my way out of this situation that's making me more uncomfortable and awkward by the second.

It's almost painful, really.

"Wynn."

"Yeah?"

"Thank you. It's not lost on me that this looks similar to the one you have of your mom's."

I can feel my heart pounding in my ears like a drum as he pulls me into his lap, wrapping me up tight.

"You're welcome," I murmur into his chest. "I know this holiday is a one-off for you, but I figured it would be a cute way for you to remember this one by."

"I could never forget you, Wynn." Logan kisses the top of my head before tucking me under his chin.

That's how we spent Christmas Day. Completely and utterly wrapped up in each other, neither of us willing to move.

It was the best Christmas I've ever had.

CHAPTER
Eighteen

WYNN

"Y ou got everything?" Logan asks as I stuff the last bag into my trunk and slam it closed.

It never fails. No matter where I go, I somehow always come back with more shit than I came with. And I'm a heavy packer, so that's saying something.

"I think so," I reluctantly answer.

My nails dig into my palms, and I fight to appear calm, praying the cracks in my voice don't betray the emotion that's begging to come out. If I had it my way, I wouldn't be leaving. It's crazy to admit this out loud, but I never felt more at home in the middle of Northern Michigan with a lumberjack man I haven't known that long than I do in Virginia with my friends I've had for years.

That's crazy, right?

What's even crazier is that if he were to ask me to stay, I would. I'd do it in a fucking heartbeat.

But he won't.

And I need to accept that.

It was fun while it lasted, but everyone knows a vacation romance has an expiration date.

"I put my number in your phone in case you need something during your drive back. If you need anything at all, don't hesitate to call me, even if you just need someone to pass the time."

Ask me to stay.

"Thanks." I smile through the pain. It's killing me, but I'm doing it. "And thank you for sticking around. You didn't have to, but I just want you to know that you made this one of the best holidays I've ever had. I'll never forget it."

Logan smiles softly at me as he wraps me up in a tight hug, holding me close like he never wants to let me go.

I sigh into his chest.

I'm going to miss this.

"Anything for you, princess." Logan's low voice vibrates against the top of my head.

My heart is shattering as I pull away from him.

As much as I want to stay in his arms, that's not my spot to claim.

"Well," I start off, but my voice sounds as watery as the emotions I'm trying so hard to hide spill into my voice. I clear my throat. "I should probably get going. I have a long drive."

Logan doesn't mutter a word as he stares at me with a look on his face I can't quite decipher. It's like he wants to say something but isn't sure if he should or not.

Ask me to stay.

He doesn't.

Instead, he reaches around me and opens my car door, shattering my heart into a million little pieces.

"Goodbye, Wynn." Logan leans in, placing one last kiss on my temple.

Ducking my head, I'm unable to meet his eye as I climb into my car for fear he will see the tears that are prickling at the corners of my eyes.

Logan slams the door shut and slaps his hand on the hood a couple of times. Another way for him to say goodbye.

I make it out onto the main road, completely out of his sight before I lose it. Full on belly rolling sobs leave my body for the next hour.

It's a miracle I could see where I was going.

And that's how I drove the entire way back to Virginia, tears streaming down my face the entire time.

I never called him, and he never called me.

It's better this way.

CHAPTER Nineteen

LOGAN

"Alright. I've had about enough of this. What's wrong with you?" my mom asks the following weekend after I watched the woman who I knew down to my bones was meant to be mine drive out of my life in a tiny fucking deathtrap.

I've been kicking myself all week for not asking her to stay.

I didn't want to hear her tell me no.

That would crush me more than seeing the tears she thought she was hiding from me streaming down her face.

"Hello? Logan?" My mom waves her hand in front of my face.

"What?" I ask, snapping out of my thoughts.

I've been in a shit fucking mood. Everyone knows it. I just can't seem to shake it.

"I asked what's wrong with you? All week you've been snapping at everyone left and right. And now you're walking around looking all sad like someone killed your puppy."

I sigh loudly as I rub my hand down my face. The last person I want to be having this conversation with is my mom.

"It's nothing. I'll get over it."

"Does it have a little something to do with Miss Wynn Anderson?" she asks with a little smirk like she knows something that I don't.

"What?" I ask, giving her my full attention.

"She was a cutie. I was hoping the two of you would hit it off," Mom says as she sets a sandwich down in front of me before pointing her finger in my direction. "And don't think I didn't notice you driving around with a gnome ornament hanging from your rearview mirror that has both of your names on it."

"Explain." I don't mean for it to come out as harsh as it does, but I'm not in the mood for a game. I'm too on edge to be embarrassed at her finding the tiny piece of herself that Wynn gave me that I want, no, need a constant reminder of.

Mom sets the dish towel down on the counter as she sighs. "I'm the one who took the booking, Logan. You know this. I saw the picture on her driver's license she had to submit with the booking. Anyone who can look that good in an ID photo, you know, is going to look amazing in person."

I'm staring at my mom like she's lost her fucking mind.

"Are you saying that you set this up?" I ask, unable to keep the shock out of my tone.

"Well, I just figured you needed a little nudge in the right direction. I mean, for goodness sake, Logan, you're in your forties and I don't have a grandchild!"

I think she's lost her fucking mind.

"How do you know she wasn't a serial killer?"

"I looked her up on social media. She seemed like a nice girl." Mom returns as if it's the most natural thing in the world.

Holy shit.

"So you set me up." It's not a question.

"Well, did you like her?" She pushes, ignoring me completely.

"Yeah, I fucking liked her. But she doesn't live here, Mom. She has a life of her own to get back to. A girl like her doesn't want to stay in an area like this with a guy like me."

"How do you know?"

"How do I know what?"

"That she wouldn't want to stay with you. Did you ask her to stay?"

No.

That's probably going to go down as one of my biggest regrets in life.

"Oh, Logan," Mom says softly as she walks over to me and places her hand on top of mine. "I'm going to hold your hand when

I say this, but you need to go get that girl and bring her home."

I swallow the lump forming in my throat. "I don't have her address."

"I do." My mom's smile is beaming like she just won the lottery. "Go get your girl."

Thirty minutes later, I'm in my truck with a weekend bag packed on my way to Virginia to bring back my girl.

CHAPTER
Twenty

WYNN

'm not proud to admit that I've spent the last week holed up in my bed, bawling my eyes out on and off as I watch The Holiday repeatedly, slowly torturing myself to death.

Every time it gets to the part where Cameron Diaz has to leave to go back to the States and she runs back to him and they live happily ever after, I lose it because I didn't get that.

I didn't go back to Logan, but he also didn't ask me to stay.

And to top it off, my boss let me go yesterday because I called in too many days in a row after just getting back from vacation. The funny thing is I don't even care. I hated that job anyway.

I sigh as I hear the doorbell chime. Heaving the covers off of me, I slowly make the trek to the front door to retrieve the food I ordered. I've ordered food all week, not being in any state to even think about cooking. My eyes have been too puffy from all the crying that I haven't even wanted to visit a drive-thru. It's pathetic, really.

The doorbell chimes again.

"I'm coming!" I yell.

Jesus Christ.

I told them to leave it at the door in the app for a reason. Why don't they ever listen?

I flip the locks and yank the door open, only to freeze. Logan stands on my porch, hands shoved in his pockets, rocking on his heels in the flannel I gave him for Christmas.

"Hey," he greets. One word ignites my body. That's the effect he has on me.

And here I am, unable to form a sentence because all I can do is stare at him in shock that he's actually here, standing on my front porch.

"Are you going to let me in?"

I step back, moving out of the doorway so Logan can pass through as I close the door behind him.

"What are you doing here?" I finally get out, suddenly extremely self-conscious about the way I look.

I'm in a pair of baggy sweatpants and t-shirt with the cuffs of the pants tucked into a pair of fuzzy socks. My hair, which I haven't brushed in days, is up in a messy bun with tendrils falling all around my face. My face is clear of makeup, and my eyes are red and puffy from crying my life away. Basically, I look amazing right now.

"Have you been crying?" he asks softly, ignoring my question completely.

"I was watching a sad movie, and it got to me," I answer, trying to cover, but anyone who took one look at me would know that's a lie. "What are you doing here?"

"I'm here for you." His response is so simple and definite.

"Me?"

"Yeah, you, princess. I'm doing what I should have done the day you left me."

"What should you have done?" I swallow.

"I should have asked you to stay."

Holy.

Shit.

My heart feels like it's going to pound out of my chest.

"Why didn't you?" I barely get out.

"I didn't think I had the right to ask that of you. It wasn't until I was home and so fucking miserable my mom had to knock some sense into me. I realized I do have that right because I've never met someone who has immediately felt like mine before."

"What are you saying?" The tightness in my chest is almost too much to take. My emotional week from hell fried my nerve endings, and I don't know how much more I can take.

"Come back to Michigan with me."

Holy shit again.

"Are you asking me or telling me?" I'm trying to keep the excitement at bay because I'm still unsure where this is going. I can't afford to get my hopes up. I don't think I'll survive if they get crushed.

"Both?" Logan smiles sheepishly. "I want you with me. I'm so wrapped up in you, princess, I can barely think straight."

"I'm wrapped up in you too," I admit, matching his smile. "How long do you want me to stay?"

"Forever." His response is instant. "I don't want to do long distance. And I sure as hell don't want to watch you drive away from me again. It about killed me."

This is everything I wanted. He's handing it to me on a silver platter. And what do I have to lose? I don't have a job anymore. Sure, Clara will miss me, but she loves to travel, so visits wouldn't be an issue.

There's nothing holding me back.

"I don't want to come on too strong and scare you off," Logan continues before pausing, taking a hesitant step toward me, mistaking my silence for not wanting to go. It never occurred to me that he would also fear rejection. "But I don't want to live my life regretting that I never told you how I feel. You're the girl I've been waiting for. I know it's soon, but I'd be a fool to let a connection like this pass by. I love you, Wynn."

"It's not too soon." Tears are pooling in the corners of my eyes. This time they're happy tears.

"It's not?" Logan's hopeful eyes are shining bright.

"No," I whisper. "It's not."

Logan's hands frame my jaw as he brings his lips to mine, sealing the deal.

"Wait," I say as I pull away, his arms moving to my waist, not wanting to let me go. "How did you find me?"

"My mom." Logan's lips tip up. "Apparently, she did some internet sleuthing when you booked the cabin and was hoping we would hit it off. She gave me your address from your booking."

A laugh bubbles out of me because what the hell. I can't wait to meet this woman.

"Is that even legal?"

"Fuck no." Logan is staring down at me, his eyes dancing. "But it led me back to you."

Unable to contain it anymore, I slam my body against Logan's, my face burrowing into his chest as he releases a grunt. His arms wrap around me, holding me tight.

"How long are you here for?" I press against his chest.

"Just the weekend. I was hoping that's all it would take to convince you to come back with me."

"Are you really sure about forever?" I hold my breath as I wait for his answer. We've only known each other for a short time, and I need to hear it again. I need to know he's taken the same nosedive into this as I have.

"I'm really sure about forever, but I'll take what I can get. I told you I have no problem waiting on you as long as you're mine."

Internally, I'm squealing.

"Let's do this."

Logan's arms convulse as he places a kiss on my temple.

I missed this.

"I know we'll have to figure out your job stuff, but I promise not to wake you up at the ass crack of dawn."

I snort. "I know you won't because you don't want me to smother you in your sleep. As far as the job thing goes… I don't have one here anymore."

Honestly, a fresh start couldn't have come at a more perfect time. It's funny how the universe has a way of working things out.

"You quit?"

"Um…not exactly. I was a little…distraught on my drive home, and that continued through the week to the point where I physically couldn't go to work. My boss basically said I wasn't pulling my weight and had no vacation days left to use, so it was either I come in or am fired."

"Why didn't you call me, princess?" Logan asks softly.

"And said what? Ask me to stay? No, thank you. I already felt like my world was ending. The thought of you rejecting me would have sent me driving off the nearest bridge."

"Never in a million years would I reject you, Wynn. Next time, call."

146

"Okay," I murmur. Tilting my head back to look at him, I notice his stubble is a bit longer, emphasizing the gray hairs on his jaw, but he remains as handsome as ever. "Want to help me pack?"

"I'll help you do anything you want if it gets your ass back to Michigan."

Logan gently taps my ass as he walks further into my house, leaving me behind.

"Thank you, Mom," I whisper to the universe.

Without her and her memory I tried to keep alive, I wouldn't have met my dream man in Northern Michigan. Cheers to farm life while wearing fur.

Epilogue

WYNN

It's been five months since Logan showed up on my doorstep and packed up everything that would fit into his truck and my car and never looked back. Clara sold all of my furniture for me and turned in the keys, telling me she's so happy I've found what I've been looking for and how I need to grab onto it.

And grab onto it I did.

Logan moved me into his house, and he hadn't been exaggerating about how spread out they all were. Each home is separated by a wide field, making it feel more like a neighborhood than one big family living on the same land. His parents live in the house Logan grew up in, which is right at the start of the driveway. Logan's follows suit with Brody's, Jackson's, and Trey's houses trailing in a line.

Every front porch overlooks a massive field that butts up to a pasture, allowing us to watch the sunset every night. It's the most gorgeous thing outside of Logan I've ever seen in my life.

His family welcomed me with open arms, and his mom took me under her wing and is showing me how to be a farmer's girlfriend, something I never thought I would be, but I wouldn't change it for the world.

ACKNOWLEDGMENTS

Mike and Odin, thank you for continuing to support me on this journey. Not everyone gets to have their dream job, and I'm incredibly grateful to you guys for helping me achieve it.

Papa, this book wouldn't have happened without the memories you helped create growing up.

Meg, thank you for reading any and every crazy bullshit I decide to write and always designing kick-ass covers for it. You're a real one.

Britt, Emily and Missi, thank you for helping make this book shine. I live for all your comments and reactions. You guys are the best.

My street team, thank you for always hyping me up. Nothing you do goes unnoticed, and I appreciate each and every one of you.

Ramona, thank you for helping me bring my book babies to life. Without you, sentences would be a jumbled mess, and commas would be missing. It's always a pleasure working with you.

ABOUT THE AUTHOR

D. Vessa is a romantic suspense author who loves a morally grey alpha, the color black and a good Aperol Spritz. She lives on the east coast with her family. When she is not writing she spends her time running from her problems, and wondering what color to dye her hair next.

www.authordvessa.com

Facebook Reader Group:
D. Vessa's Twisted Little Ravens

ALSO BY D. VESSA